Stephen Graham was born in London, England and continues to live in London. This metaphorically written crime novel tells the tale of the rough streets of London upon which Stephen grew. Previously involved in gang related activities Stephen managed to turn his life around, with determination and focus he successfully attained a medical degree in Sports Rehabilitation at university.

This book was not written with intent to glorify violence, but rather to give a realistic insight to the consequences that can occur as a result of gun/knife crime and gang related activity, as well as the devastation it causes to families and communities. Please bear in mind as you read this book the addictive hold weapons of offensive have upon our youth, and the importance of knowing and loving self as a means to implement change.

Email - Stephen@expressivelypassionate.com
Twitter - @StephenGGraham
Facebook – fb.me/authorstephengraham

You can purchase other books written by Stephen Graham from www.expressivelypassionate.com

I'm a Gun
By Stephen Graham

Expressively Passionate publications

First published in 2012 by Expressively Passionate Publications

ISBN-13: 978-1-62209-449-3

Copyright © Stephen Graham, 2012

The right of Stephen Graham to be identified as the author of this book has been asserted by him in accordance with the Copyright, Designs and Patents Acts 1988.

This book is the work of fiction. Names, characters, and incidences are products of the author's imagination or are used fictitiously. Any resemblance of actual events, locations or actual people's lives, living or dead is entirely coincidental.

All rights reserved. No reproduction, copy or transmission of this publication may be used without written permission. No paragraph of this book may be reproduced, copied or transmitted without written permission or in accordance with the provisions of the copyright act.

Any person who does any unauthorised act in relation to this publication may be liable to criminal prosecution and civil claims for damage.

Printed and bound in the USA

This book is sold subject to the conditions that it shall not, by way of trade or otherwise, be lent, re-sold, hired out, or otherwise circulated without prior consent from the publisher in any form of binding and cover than that in which it is published and without a similar condition being imposed on the subsequent purchaser.

Barely alive, Blacka lay bleeding from a stab wound to his stomach, and gunshot wounds to his chest and abdomen. Gasping for breath, his chest rose and dropped rapidly as blood poured from his torn flesh. His lips unable to close as blood filled his mouth blocking his airways, with every cough, clots of blood spewed from his mouth. A combination of saliva mixed with thick, dark, discoloured blood produced a sticky fluid which dribbled from the corner of his mouth. As he choked on his own blood, Blacka's body fluids became his greatest obstacle, he struggled to breathe and in desperation he gasped for air.

One would think he would have come to grips with death, after seeing many fall by the simple movement of his trigger finger during the period I allowed him to reign terror.

Amazed at his foolish heart, how easily misled is man. I stared at him as he lay on the cold concrete, his garments drenched in his own blood, in my direction he gazed. I looked into his dull eyes; his eyes showed betrayal and disappointment, he felt betrayed.

They say if you make a deal with the devil, he'll give you your heart's desire at a price. Well I am just as evil, even as great, why, because you do a deal with the evil you can see, by believing in me, I give you power and false security, I am the master of illusions. Consciously I am your servant providing you do my evil deeds; subconsciously I am your master.

The devils greatest trick was to convince the world that he didn't exist, mine is simple, let you believe you have power, let your ego lead you, for God hates ego, but me, I hate God.

Crown me king of the streets, I was made to kill, to be concealed, so niggas carry me under their clothes, not willing to expose me until I am ready to fulfil my part of the bargain, the thing is, I'm loyal to no man. Blacka bears witness of my truth, I promise eternal life to no-one, I wasn't made to be loved, and neither will I give love. Let me introduce myself, I am a motherfucking Gun.

Let me take you back in time….

Chapter 1

It all begins somewhere

Ten months ago

"Yo, wa gwan?" said Blacka with a smile as he approached his sisters front door.

"Deya," replied Danger. "Yo, blacks follow mi up di road?"

"What you up to?"

"Movements," Danger replied.

"I'm not stopping still, jus come to hail you and sis, and check my nephew."

"Sun ah beam my yout come mek we touch da road," he smiled. "Gangsta yu ah come?"

"Yeah cool, I'm jus gonna hail up sis, and Melekiah."

"Inna di cyar mi deh." Danger walked off.

"Cool." Blacka responded as he walked towards the front door. Minutes later the horn beeped. "So where we going," Blacka asked as he opened the car door.

"Where you two off to?" Cassandra shouted as she stood at the front door, holding Dangers son in her hand.

"Soon come sis, following Danger up the road."

"Danger where you going, you gonna be long? Cassandra asked.

"Soon come, wi ah go ah Harlesden and come back, might pass South Kilburn, link my yout and forward come. Nah tek long," Danger responded.

"You two be careful," said Cassandra.

"Man always careful," Danger reassured her.

Cassandra walked up to the car. "You guys don't have anything on you do you? Be careful I mean it, all day sirens have been going off."

"Wa'appen to yuh," he smiled. "No watch nuttin baby, man gud, man always careful."

"So you're not carrying Danger?" She looked at her brother also, "Either of you?"

"Nah sis," Blacka responded as he played with Melekiah's hand through the open car window.

"Mi nah have nuttin pon mi, wi soon come." Danger blew her a kiss.

"I mean it Danger."

He laughed before saying "Cool nah babes, mi soon come."

"Daddy can I come?" asked Melekiah. "Please."

"Take him wid you if you're jus going Harlesden den?

"Melekiah mi soon come, when mi come back, mi and yuh uncle ah go tek yu park, yeah."

"Okay Daddy," he smiled. "Love you daddy."

"Love yuh too. Leaning his head to one side he winked at Cassandra. "Soon come baby."

Danger beeped as he pulled away. As they drove down the road Danger laughed, Blacka turned and responded to his laugh. "What?"

"Yuh sista blud, ah gud gal, man rate her, she nah inna di ediat ting, anyhow she kno seh mi ave it pon mi ah one bag ah arms house fi mi leave." He laughed again. "Dats why I rate her, she no deh pon di image, nor hype ting, she jus easy. Ah jus true she love man still, an how man deal wid her an di yout. Dun kno mi ah family man, an love di family life, ah jus true ah survival and man come ah England and no really ave certain tings, yuh dun come ah yard and see how di ting set pon di ends. No job nah deh, no opportunity nah deh inna di garrison. Ah one life mi kno, worst mi papers nah come true yet, an mi can't sit down an jus look pon life go by, mi haffi hustle. Man ah shotta, dats all mi kno, dat is who mi is."

"I feel you darg."

"Mi no love lie to yuh sista still, but yu kno mi nah left it. Mi nah left mi gun. Speaking of gun, yu and yuh fren dem deh pon sum mad ting, unno ah share di gun dem amongst one a nadda like a dutty gal or a bag ah sweetie, and yu kno wa'appen when yu fuck wid a dutty gal don't? Yu catch wa yu nah waan." Blacka laughed. "Yuh duppy any ting yet?

"Won't lie to you fams, I ain't killed no-one, nor shot anyone, but if it comes to it, you know I would." Blacka responded firmly.

"Dun kno yu ave it inna yuh, and dat is why mi nah really wa yuh inna it. No gud nah inna it my yout, wid guns come death, whether it's sum'ady else or yu, death ah come. One ting mi learn ah yard growing up, shotta code teaches gunshot no respect no man."

"Any man can die blud, for real."

"Nah jus any man, if yu inna di gun ting mek yuh mind up fi dead, so when death come yu welcome it, like sum fat pussy gal. Die gracefully."

Danger looked at Blacka with a smile. Blacka stared at Danger. Danger laughed, Blacka turned away and began to think.

After making their stop in Harlesden, they continued their journey to Kilburn. As they drove down the Harrow Road the sound of a siren and flashing lights caught their attention causing both Danger and Blacka to look through the rear view mirror at the police car that trailed them.

"Yo Blacka, mi ah gi yuh di gun, hear wah yu do. When mi turn into the road, mi ah gwaan like mi aguh stop, yuh see when him get outta di cyar and walk towards wi, mi ah drive off, an yuh see once we outta him sight mi wah yuh jus jump out, lay low or run, which eva betta. Mi will gwaan drive." Danger handed me over to him. "Hold dis."

I felt Blacka's heart beat as his trembling hands held me, the pulse in his finger declared his fear, adrenaline pumped through his blood, his racing heart beat thumped beneath his chest.

Danger pulled up as he turned onto Ashmore road, as the cop car pulled up the officer got out, the sound of Dangers tyres as they drove off gave a loud scream. "Now," shouted Danger.

As they turned the corner, Blacka jumped out and hid behind a car as they turned the corner. The cop car came speeding around the corner in pursuit of Danger, unaware of what had just occurred, Blacka kept low and out of sight. As the cop car disappeared Blacka stood up and walked to a friend's house that lived on the estate off Ashmore Road. He knew it was only a matter of minutes before the streets were fumigated with po-po, and he had every intention not to get caught.

Later that night Danger had been charged for failing to stop and was released from the police station. They say disasters come in three's, but what Blacka and his family were about to encounter was the unthinkable.

Chapter 2

The turning point

Blacka sat in his sister's living room listening to her go on and on. Cassandra had called him on his mobile an hour ago and told him to find his black arse round her yard, and explained she had just spoken to Danger's solicitor. Unwilling to talk on the phone, Blacka had made haste only to encounter his sister in distress once again and wanted to leave as he had done before.

Earlier that day he had left Cassandra's house after telling her what had happened, which led to them arguing, even though he denied any knowledge of Danger carrying heat prior to the moment the police car pulled them over, which wasn't exactly true, but now wasn't the time or moment to say otherwise, for he knew he wouldn't hear the last of it.

As they sat there waiting for Danger to walk through the door, Blacka thought to himself how much he was glad he wasn't in Danger's shoes right now.

Cassandra was outraged, the fact that her and Danger had worked so hard to establish a decent home, herself a good job, their wedding which had taken place in Jamaica, his legal papers which they were working on, and the thought of him blowing everything by being so careless made her angry. What made things worse was that he had lied to her about carrying his gun. Now, the fact that he had not too long called and said he was going to link his key brethren Shaggy, who lived on the South Kilburn estate before coming straight home, only made her more angry, Cassandra, was furious.

Shaggy and Danger were extremely close from back home; they had survived the trenches of Jamaican ghetto life together, and would ride and die for one another. If it was a different occasion altogether, Cassandra wouldn't be so angry, I guess the thought of what had just happened really upset her. Knowing that Danger still chose to roam the streets after putting himself, her little brother, not to mention their future at risk. When considering her reasons for being angry, think about it, she was beyond furious.

I listened from beneath Blacka's sweaty garment at Cassandra shouting and cursing. If only she could understand his mentality; If only she could comprehend the reason why he always chose to carry me. Danger was mentally in love with us both. That's right he shares her with me. We both have the power to please him, to arouse him, the only difference is, she helped him to bring life into the world, whereas I, well, I helped him to take it.

Cassandra only grew more frustrated and angry as she waited for Danger to come home. I listened as she cursed and called him a heartless, selfish, idiot and for a moment wondered if she knew the Danger I knew, but was unable to see the reflection I saw in the mirror. The words she spoke were out of anger; she had not known Danger's anger on which I was fuelled. In darkness I was hidden from Cassandra's eyes as I listened to her mumble on, but then also was the Danger I knew, hidden from Cassandra's eyes. His dark side she had never seen, he lived two separate lives so perfectly. The sweet husband and baby daddy when in her presence, then the ruthless killer, once he stepped through that door and united with his boys. She had heard things and he had told her of his past life in Jamaica, blinded by love she believed in a future where they would both move away from the ends, far away from Harlesden and relocate in a new area, both find jobs and enjoy a fresh start. I had heard Danger promise her this and more, once his papers came through. Only if it were possible, I would have never allowed Danger to give me up. You see, Danger fuelled me, his touch; his hands smelled of death, spoiled by blood, weeping souls rested not. I wasn't prepared to let Danger dash me to the curb, after all, I made him powerful, gave him street credit, made him feared, and exalted his name. To repay me in such a manner would show no gratitude. I would unfortunately have to cut him down and give his strength unto another. Well, we'll cross that path when it comes, hopefully it doesn't' come, and then Danger will never know what will be the bitter ending to a long companionship turned sour. It would be such a shame if we became foe.

"Where's his keys, he's forgotten his key, ediat." Cassandra said as she walked to the door. "It's for you," she said as she walked back into the living room. "He's fuckin lucky it wasn't him, he's talkin the piss now. I'm really pissed off wid him."

"Wa gwan bruv?" Blacka said as he stood at the door.

"Come," his friend took a step back, and put his finger on his lip signifying Blacka to be silent.

"What?" asked Blacka as he became agitated and serious, snapping at his friend. "I'm not in the mood for fuckin games blud. What?"

"Bruv, I don't want Cassandra hear. Jus come."

"What?" asked Blacka.

"Dem pussies killed Danger blud."

"What da fuck you sayin? What da fuck, don't fuck around." Blacka went quite for a second. "Dean, don't be fuckin talkin shit blud. Yo blud, what da fuck you talkin' about?

"My cousin jus holla at me and told me those niggas over East jus killed Danger. He said there was a shoot out between Danger and Shaggy and some yardies. He said he heard that Shaggy was bussin it, but Danger wasn't, and during the shoot out Danger must have run the opposite way from Shaggy innit, and they must have catch up to him and shot him up. Blud I'm fuckin' pissed."

"Oh shit, fuck."

"Blud what I don't understand is Danger don't left it, he's always got his ting blud."

"I got his fuckin ting."

"What you mean you got his fuckin ting blud?"

"Today we almost got shift blud wid da strap. I jumped out and hid and Danger drove off. The police charged Danger for failing to stop, now fuckin dis. Shit, sis is gonna go mad. What the fuck is he doing going over East? He told her he soon come home, he said he's checking Shaggy at his yard in Kilburn and then coming straight. He knew she was pissed already, and then he fuckin goes East and give his life away. How the fuck am I gonna tell her dis?" Blacka said angrily.

"Tell me what?" said Cassandra. "What?"

"Sis come we go inside."

"Talk to me. What? What, talk then?"

"It's Danger," said Blacka and then bit his lip as he looked down at the floor.

"What about Danger?" Cassandra replied, looking angry, yet confused.

Blacka went silent.

"Dean, what, you and Blacka discussing Danger outside my house, what has Danger done now, I swear when he gets in I am gonna kill him. What has he done?"

Dean looked at Blacka. Blacka looked at his sister and then again he looked down at the floor before looking up at the moon which shone in the clear dark skies. "Sis, Danger's dead," Blacka said as he looked down at the floor before looking at Cassandra.

"What?" she responded. "Dean is that what you both were outside my house talking about?" she asked very calmly.

Dean stood there in silence. Blacka likewise, they both knew her reaction wasn't natural.

"Dean, I would like you to move from in front of my house please, you too Blacka. Please leave." Her voice remained calm.

Within seconds of speaking, Cassandra was about to collapse when Blacka caught her. Dean assisted and they brought Cassandra into the house. All night Cassandra mourned as she held Melekiah tightly in her arms. By this time Dean had gone home. While he was there he had told them all he knew, everything that his cousin had told him.

Blacka sat there in silence, tears rolled down his cheek he couldn't believe Danger had been killed and robbed of his chain and watch. I felt Blacka's hand press against me as he sat there and thought about what Dean had told them. If only he was with Danger thought Blacka the outcome may have been different. Angered and upset Blacka stood up, "Sis do you want me to stay the night?"

"Why? Where you going?" Cassandra asked.

"Nowhere, home, why, where do you think I'm going?"

"Blacka please, I can't lose you as well."

"Sis, you're not gonna lose me."

"Stay in Melekiah's room, he'll sleep wid me tonight. I can't sleep anyway," she said as tears rolled down her cheek onto Melekiah's clothes as he lay sleeping in her arms.

Blacka looked at Melekiah sleeping, and shook his head. "Cool." Blacka walked towards the living room door. "I'm going upstairs."

Blacka closed Melekiah's bedroom door as he stepped in and stood against it. Blacka had no more tears to give, tears were unable to flow from his eyes, yet he cried. Consumed and filled with anger, frustrated he wished only to be there with Danger at the time of the shoot out. Blacka walked towards the bed, as he did so he took me out and threw me on the bed and then sat down. As he sat there and thought, he looked at me. "Why didn't he come back for his ting, man jus dash way his life. Fuck," said Blacka in an almost whispering tone.

I honestly don't think Blacka meant to speak out loud, but he was right. If Danger had me with him they would have faced our wrath. Danger's carelessness caused him to lose his life, without me he's nothing; he should have never forgotten that.

As Blacka sat there thinking, unable to come to grips with the demise of his good friend and brother in law, again the thoughts of me protecting Danger crossed his mind. I knew these were his thoughts as he stared at me the whole time. Undoubtedly he was right, I have the capability to protect in the streets, yet neither he nor Danger or anyone one else who has had me in their possession ever wondered why and how I was put on the streets. What good cometh of me, my soul purpose is to cause death, I am an enemy even to myself, for the fact I despise the image of my creator. I was created by man, yet I influence the mind of the very image that created me, man is but a fool.

With his sleeve Blacka wiped the snot from his nose and then picked me up, the feeling of innocence surrounded me. His touch was that of a virgin, his hands were pure; they had never seen blood, well not yet at least. I have felt many hands like these and have removed the innocence from them, staining them, washing them in the blood of man, removing their purity and giving them new life, a dark road on the path to nowhere.

Turning me back and forth Blacka looked at me, his stare was intense, the pulse in his fingers increased as his heart pumped forth blood, he desired blood, he desired the blood of those who had ripped his family apart, and I desired Blacka's soul.

Put your trust in me, give yourself to me and I will help thee and avenge thy enemies.

Chapter 3

Vengeance comes at a price

A week later

"Wa gwan Dean?" Said Blacka as he answered his mobile phone. "What you sayin family?"

"Yo Blacks where you at?"

"In Stonebridge wid Shaggy, soon come back to Church Road blud, why, what's up?"

"My cousin jus told me he knows where to find those fuckin yardies who killed fambo blud."

"Say no more, where you at?

"On the block."

"Be there in a hot minute blud."

"Cool."

"You sure it's dem?" asked Blacka as he approached Dean.

"Bruv, man's wearing the watch, you feel me."

"I say we roll pon di bwoy dem an dun dem bloodclaat," said Shaggy. "Dem pussy anna bad man ah yard, ah England dem come an buss gun. Ah lock dem lock gun fi man ah yard, ah wi ah di shotta. Dem kno mi and Danger ah killa fi dem. Dem dun mi fren, mi ah go kill everyone one of dem bloodclaat. Ah true dem see seh Danger nah buss it di night deh, ah mi alone ah buss it up pon dem mad. If Danger did have it, or if him neva did run off." Shaggy took a deep breath, a tear rolled down his cheek. "Mi ah kill every bloodclaat one ah dem."

"We need to catch dem off guard bruv, they're always packing heat, man ain't looking to have a shoot out ting blud, dats bait. Mans looking to jus kill dem, get away, all of us you feel me," said Dean."

"So what's your cousin sayin?" asked Blacka.

"He sayin dat one of the main niggas for their crew lives on his estate, and they're always around there especially when suns hot, they're out there playin dominos and shit, you kno how dem yardies do already."

"Cool." Responded Blacka as he bit his lip and nodded his head.

"Cuz is sayin dat da goons over there will move to dem, jus say the word. My cousin dem don't really like dem still, jus true they ain't got no beef wid dem until now. You kno every man rate Danger blud."

"Nah, tell dem man cool blud, we're doing it, I'm killin dem pussies myself," said Blacka. "Fuck dat, I'm killin dem niggas."

"Fi real Blacka, mi wah look inna man face wen dem ah dead." Shaggy added.

"We don't have to carry heat, jus drive over, when we get to East, Price and his peeps will give us straps. So we jus do what we're doing an come back, yu feel me."

"Fuck dat, I'm blastin niggas wid Danger's gun bruv, I'm travelling strapped, fuck dat."

"Fuck it den, we're all travelling strapped," said Dean.

"Dis is for Danger blud." Shaggy said as he looked up at the skies. "Tonight mi ah go show dem who ah di real killa."

"Let me holla at my cousin first." Dean took out his phone and made his call. "Yo cuz, I'm wid Blacka and Shaggy, man wah do dis ting tonight blud?" Dean nodded repeatedly as he listened to his cousin. "Yeah, yeah, yeah, safe, yeah, don't need it. Say no more."

"What's he sayin?" asked Blacka.

"He's sayin tonight's good, he said about eleven, cause man rave; so man will be in their yard chillin, sleepin, whateva innit. You kno how dem man don't leave their yard til early morning, catch a nigga slippin. He asked if we need heat, told him we don't need it. He said he's comin on the works blud. I told him safe."

"Cool, respect." Blacka responded.

Later that night Blacka, Dean, Shaggy and Dean's cousin Price and a gorgeous looking girl who Price introduced as Miss Peng approached the yardie man's door.

"You know what to do babe," said Price.

She walked up to the door and rang the bell. Blacka and others stood at each side of the door."

18

"Ah who dat?"

"Hi is Tracy there please?"

"No Tracy no live ya."

"Sorry to botha you, do you know which house she lives at?"

Knowing he could see her through the key hole they depended on him to be lured in by her sweet voice and pretty face, and they were right.

"Tracy, mi nah kno Tracy, but I..." he said as he opened the door smiling.

Before he could say another word Price kicked the door on him as he attempted to shut it, and opened fire hitting him in his chest and piercing a whole in his sternum. Shaggy fired two shots into his torso as he lay on the floor.

Blacka rushed in behind them, his hand felt extremely warm as he gripped me tightly. He pointed me at a man who stood in the passage near the living room door. The stranger turned to run. The scent of my aroma as Blacka pulled the trigger filled the hallway with the crime of passion. Untamed and viciously I attacked him from behind boring into his back like a pit bull terrier, locking and lodging into his spine, he fell to the ground instantly. Blacka kicked him in his face. At that moment Blacka had given his heart to me, I knew as he stood over the man, smiled and then bit his lip as he ordered me to enter his face. From an angle, copper from my body smashed through his eye socket and came out through the other side of his skull, chipping into the laminated flooring.

Oh Blacka's adrenaline aroused me, I had found companionship again. I had introduced another to the path of death, his hands felt better than Danger's, oh they were much better; these once pure hands had now been stained, unlike Danger's whose hands were covered with the blood of man when we met, Blacka was a virgin and I had taken his purity, his virginity, he would never forget me. For what man forgets his first……

Price and Dean kicked at the kitchen door. "Wa di bloodclaat, wa di fuck unno wa kill mi!" shouted a man from behind the door as he braced against it. A woman screamed.

"Open the fuckin door," said Dean.

"Kill the bitch too," said Blacka as he walked up to the kitchen door.

Shaggy and Price opened fire letting off multiple shots at the door. Shaggy gave the door one kick, it flew open. On the floor lay a man bleeding from his shoulder and chest. The lady also had a gunshot wound to her shoulder. She stood in the back of the kitchen screaming.

"Shut your fuckin mout before I shut it for you." Blacka said as he stepped into the kitchen, he looked at the man's wrist. His eyes turned dark red as he stared at Dangers watch.

He gripped me tighter, I felt desired. I felt wanted and was more than willing to satisfy his hunger for blood.

"You're wearing my fams watch blud," he said as he pointed me at my target.

"Tek it my yout, tek it, don't kill mi, anno mi do it, man owe mi sum money an gi mi fi di money weh him owe mi."

"Take it off and throw it on the fuckin floor you punk." Blacka had no desire for physical contact; he was angry, raged, but not stupid. He had no intention of leaving evidence for forensics.

"See it deh."

"Pussy wa yuh seh, anno yu," said Shaggy as he stood next to Blacka.

"Shaggy don't kill mi." The man began crawling backwards. "Ah yard di whole ah wi ah come from, spare mi nah gangsta."

"Pussy stand next to ya gal," said Shaggy. "Bitch, help him up."

Dean and Price stood beside Shaggy and Blacka. As the woman helped him to his feet, Blacka looked at Shaggy, who looked to his left at Dean and Price. Blacka's blood was still pumping with adrenaline and I loved every second of it. His mind was totally focused as he thought about one specific small area on his body. The blood vessels in his arm sent blood pouring into his hand and down towards his trigger finger.

Against the wall the yardie leaned as his girlfriend held him trying to contain her fear, she cried.

"Don't kill mi, at least mek di gal live rude bwoy."

"Live." Shaggy said as he raised his gun.

Dean, Price and Blacka raised theirs also. Suddenly the man pulled the lady in front of him as they opened fire. Both the man and women fell to the floor. Instantly she died, she had taken multiple shots to her upper body and head.

Being in the wrong place at the wrong time, and dating the wrong kind of man had cost an innocent woman her life.

Blacka walked up to him as he lay their bleeding to death. He was moments away from knowing what lies beyond the physical realm, for them the wait was too long. Blacka pointed me at him; there I go again illuminating the room with the sweet aroma somewhat pleasant like personified perfume. The others joined in, emptying their clips, they filled his body with bullets, like a Sunday roast they stuffed him with copper, and copper jacketed hollow points before fleeing the scene.

Back in the manor the four of them sat in Dean's yard smoking and drinking.

"Gi me some of the zoot blud," said Dean."

"You jus skin up blud, smoked a fat zoot, and you now want some of mine, fuck you blud, you're a greedy nigga." Blacka responded and laughed.

Dean laughed.

"Rap up a ting nah my yout, see weed." Shaggy said.

"Shaggy, you shouldn't even give him weed. Fuckin weed head."

"Fuck you Price, you better jump in a fuckin cab home you cunt." Dean responded. "Make your fuckin way back to East you bitch, or sleep outside wid my fuckin dog."

Everyone laughed including Price.

"Fuck you cuz." Price replied as he laughed.

"Nah I'm fuckin wid you cuz, you're my nigga for life," said Dean as he built his zoot.

"On the real still, when I leave Church Road, I'm heading Harlesden blud, I'm gonna fuck that freaky bitch, she's a slut I swear down blud, she nasty."

"An yu ah go fuck her?" Shaggy asked.

"Course, she should run a school, she's a fuckin headmaster."

Shaggy spat out his Hennessy as he laughed, everyone burst out laughing.

"Bumbaclaat. Headmaster da man call her," Shaggy said aloud. Everyone continued to laugh. "Di man say headmaster, bumbaclaat star man nah easy."

"Dean ain't her head game of the chain."

"Don't involve me blud."

"So wah, Dean, she gi yu head too?" Shaggy asked as he laughed.

"Dats what I'm sayin blud, these fuckin dumb girls, she had me and my cuz giving us both heads in the yard, she's a hoe."

"Call her before you leave out fams," said Blacka.

Price laughed before saying, "Did dat when we were in East blud."

"You fuckin nasty guy," said Dean. "I was wondering why you came down."

"Fuck you," Price kept laughing.

"Suckin off cousin, one after anotha, and then these bitches wonder why man diss up their bloodclaat, and treat dem like fuckin hoes." Blacka stated. "Joker, after being known as a slapper whose gonna settle down wid dem. You settle down wid dem kind of gyal, an you settle down with every fuckin nigga in da hood blud."

Everyone laughed.

I was proud of Blacka, I thought Blacka was handling it well, he seemed relaxed. The thought of what had taken place over in East London seemed not to be on his mind, his energy felt calm, his breathing registered normal. However, the night was still early, and Blacka was yet to be alone. How he felt over the following days, especially nights were going to tell Blacka's true state of mind.

"Hoes will be hoes. You can't turn a hoe into a house wife," said Dean and laughed. "So don't try cuz."

"Fuck off you dick head," responded Price as he laughed.

Everyone laughed.

They continued to smoke, drink, joke and laugh a little while longer before they called it a night and everyone went their own way.

At home, Blacka sat in his living room watching TV and drinking a glass of juice as the buzz started to fade and loneliness kicked in. Blacka began to reminisce on Danger and what had just taken place over in East London.

His pulse began to slow down, as he breathed Blacka had gone into deep thought, he became unnaturally relaxed, then suddenly his pulse increased back to normal and then slightly beyond.

Blacka stood up, turned the TV off, put the glass in the kitchen and then walked into his bedroom.

As he entered, he took me out of his waist and held me in his hand and did the same thing as he had done the night he had found out about Danger's death; he turned me back and forth as he stared at me.

The pulse in his hands gave indication of a slight increase, but it wasn't that which warmed the oil in my chamber and empowered the spring in my magazine, it was his grip, his blood stained hands desired more blood; like a vampire he would never be full, I knew I was creating a beast, a dark form of nature, an evil subject to do my desire. Blacka was going to continue where Danger had left off; in fact he was going to surpass his killing instinct.

The following night Blacka sat in his sister's living room holding his nephew in his arms, watching a movie with his sister. He had been there all evening, since sharing a family dinner.

"He's sleeping bruv. You staying the night or you going home?" asked Cassandra.

"Going home sis."

"Put him in his room then. Thanks."

Blacka kissed him on his forehead and then stood up. He carried him up stairs and into his bedroom. Blacka laid Melekiah in his bed and covered him with his sheet. Blacka sat there looking at his nephew as he slept. Danger came to mind as Blacka did what he would usually do. "Your daddy's spirit can rest now, they got what they deserved." Blacka said in an almost whispering tone, as he looked at Melekiah sleeping. "Your father loved you; he will always love you and watch over you." He kissed him again on his forehead. The feeling of Blacka's lips on his nephew's forehead caused Melekiah to turn in his sleep.

Blacka took a deep breath and exhaled his tension into the air. He loved his nephew, and hated the thought of him growing up without his father.

As he sat there Cassandra came into the room. "I thought you got lost," she smiled. Seeing the look on his face, hers changed also. "Bro I need to ask you something, be honest with me. There was a multiple murder over East London last night. Some yardies and a lady were killed. Tell me it's got nothing to do wid you?"

He shook his head as if to say no.

She looked him in his eyes, "You being honest wid me right?"

"Yeah." He smiled. "Nah sis, it's got nuttin to do wid me."

"Revenge isn't always the answer you know dat right. Leave vengeance to God. You know if mum was here she would have said da same thing to you."

"I hear you sis, its nuttin to do wid me. I'm jus thinking about being here for little man, you feel me."

"Well he needs dat male figure in his life."

"And I'll be there sis."

Cassandra held her arms open. Blacka stood up and embraced his sister. He hated the thought of deceiving her, but then he knew he was unable to tell her the truth.

Chapter 4

The dark side

3 months later

"Wa gwan cuz?" Dean said excitedly as Blacka approached. "Bruv, bruv, shit." Dean bursted out laughing as he embraced Blacka. "Billy the kid nigga."

Blacka laughed.

"You're going all out blud, like you're on some mad mission."

"What you talkin bout," Blacka had a smile on his face as he responded. "What kind of mission fams?"

Dean pulled Blacka away from the crowd. "You took dat yout hostage, and when his fren dem paid you, the next day you kidnapped him again blud."

Blacka put his hand over his mouth as he laughed. "Oh dat, dats double pay bro." He kissed his teeth. "Fuck dem."

"What, you think I didn't know." Dean said as he smiled. "So what you up to today fams? What's the plan?"

"Nuttin, jus chillin blud. Why, wa gwan?"

"Jus here fams, yo famo," Dean laughed before he continued to talk. "Your name's ringin blud, for the last couple month's blud you've been going on dark. Man dem out there fear you, their shook, trust me."

"Fuckin right to be, I'm gonna fuckin rob every one of those pussies."

"I feel you."

"Hold dis Dean." Blacka took out a wad of money, peeled off the rubber band and gave Dean half. "You're my nigga foreva, even when you don't see me I'm always there bruv, a phone call away you get me."

Dean nodded. "Got yuh back darg, you know dat."

"Come man lets go back over there wid the rest of the goons."

Blacka had found a dark side to his self that now changed his very perception of a true street solider. It also changed how people around him, and those who encountered our wrath perceived him. The domino effect of the reincarnated Blacka spread both near and far, together we were a force to be reckoned with. I had made Blacka a menace to society, he was considered more than an outcast to London's working society. His loyalty was to a few, and his acquaintances grew slim.

In his delusional mind he loved me, and preferred the companionship of cold steel over mortal flesh. Blacka was spending more time with me, than anyone else. Deep down Blacka felt he needed no-one but me, you see, I showed him strength and made him feel stronger than any man could ever do.

I caused people to fear him, I gave him power on the streets, his heart was growing as dark as my steel frame. His mind began to work like my creator who created me, his notion was simple; one man is more powerful with me, than many without me. Because of me, Blacka was fearless, and therefore saw no reason to roll with two or three goons on a job, when rolling with me was equal to thirteen powerful dudes more stronger than bodybuilders, more vicious than lions and faster than the swift eagle; not to mention if he required I could carry an extra man, making it thirteen in the magazine and one in the head. Together we were a small army, a crew all to ourselves. Blacka and I were perfect for one another.

Blacka and Dean had sent two of their soldiers to the shop to get some liquor. Blacka chilled with the goons from the area for just over an hour drinking and smoking. They laughed and joked around and just talked, this was typical for a hot day on the block. But hanging out wasn't one of Blacka's most pleasurable joys anymore; he had found joy and comfort doing other things. It was time to leave and pick up his whip. Blacka had other agendas to attend to and places to be.

"Man dem gone. Dean, link you up likkle more." Blacka turned to walk. "Bless," he said as he walked off with his hand in the air.

Later that evening, Blacka sat on his bed with me at his side counting the thousands we had just made, £11,275 in cash to be precise and a sports bag filled with weed delighted his hands which now smelt of death, Blacka smiled.

Dipping into the bag he took out a small bud crumbled it and began to build a zoot. Grinning he felt pleased as he inhaled the weed and looked at the cash which he had thrown on the bed.

Blacka lay back on the bed and looked up at the ceiling as he started to think about the first time he had ever killed anyone, and why. A tear came to his eye as he thought about Danger.

Months had gone by and to Blacka it seemed like yesterday. Danger was more than a brother-in-law to him; he was a close friend, someone in whom Blacka would confide. His love for Danger was unconditional, although Danger was a shotta, and a dangerous one at that, he was a family man, a people's person, who was much loved and respected by many of the young and elderly people in their community as well as in numerous other areas. Danger was renowned for putting on treats for kids, such as fun days and community barbecues, as well as some of the best bashment dances and stage shows.

Blacka smiled as he thought about Danger's mixed personalities. What really caused him to smile was the fact that he knew it was that which drew him to Danger and the fact that Danger would not only school him about street life, but encourage him to go and do a course, or look work, or go do something with himself.

The fact that Danger would encourage him to make something of himself, and explain that if he had the opportunity to get free education, or have the chance for government to pay for him to do a course, he would jump at it. Reminiscing on such thoughts only reassured Blacka how much Danger loved, respected and only wished the best for him. But Blacka being Blacka, college and university weren't gonna make him fast bucks to live financially like how Danger lived, and he wanted that money lifestyle now.

He thought about what people had said that when you kill someone for the first time you experience sleepless nights; living the experience himself Blacka wasn't in agreement. He had thought about it a few days later, but sleep wasn't a problem for Blacka, he slept peacefully like a dream, with me under his mattress.

That night in East London, I had given Blacka his first taste of the power which I clothed in illusion; the feeling of invincibility. Blacka had sought my help and willingly I obliged. I am faithful to anyone who is willing to kill their conscience disregard respect for human life and walk upon the destructive path.

Blacka sat up and built another zoot, as he sat there puffing away like a dragon, fire in his eyes, the stare of death and dark thoughts comforted his troubled soul, not that Blacka thought there was anything strange about his new found passion.

Blacka picked up the remote for his system, pressed play and then threw it on the bed. He took off his top and then began nodding his head to the bass of the gangster rap tune that thumped from his speakers, he went down onto the floor with the zoot in his mouth and begun to do press-ups.

"Keep da chest pumped." Blacka got up and looked in the mirror. "Summer look, yeah nigga." He picked me up off the bed. "Dis is my baby here, she's shooting niggas and there ain't no mudafuckin cure in da clinic when she touch a nigga." He stared at me through the mirror as he swayed from side to side as he listened to the music.

I always wonder why black males found so much pride in the use of a word initially used to belittle them, and yet now free they have taken it unto themselves as if psychologically they still desired to be slaves. But hey, as they say, there's nothing more self-destructive then an ignorant black man with a gun in his hand.

It's amazing how the human mind can be easily influenced and controlled; how people can be manipulated without truly acknowledging and knowing they are being controlled, yet if told so would be in denial.

I have listened to many gangster rap songs and not once have I heard a song say kill a cracker, shoot the white man. Everyone seems to say the same thing, kill a nigga. If gangster rap isn't self destructive to the black community and a boost to my creator's economy then I am delusional myself.

I contemplated if it was the weed talking or as they say when you're drunk or high you are your true self. Blacka spoke and acted with total commitment to being a servant to his master who in turn is a servant to man. That evening he had named me the army, I was his whole platoon. Dark projections formed images in Blacka's mind as he stood there before the mirror with me in his hand. By his firm grip, I felt a place of belonging in his heart, we were knitted to destruction. In the mirror he danced for a while entertaining us both before he sat down and rolled up another zoot. Blacka lit it, took a drag and then picked up his phone, turned the music down and made a call. "Wa gwan cuz?"

"What you sayin Blacks?"

"I'm good cuz. I got a sports bag full of your ting. Yu gonna come for it?"

"You're eatin everyting cuz, you ain't playin out here."

"Don't seek don't eat nigga, an I'm eatin mudafuckas. I eat niggas." Blacka gave off a false laugh. "So do you want it?"

"Course."

"Yu comin to get it or what?"

"Bring it over blud."

"Bonso you mad, I ain't comin over South now. How's da fams, how's aunty anyway?"

"She's good blud, were all good. Da man dem been asking for you, Cha Chu, Prince, Blue, Ticka, everyone blud, no one ain't seen a nigga since Danger's funeral. But man dem hearing blud, you're jacking everything. The dudes you jacked over these sides last month somehow one of dem found out you're my cousin innit, and spoke to my sista an she gave mi his number, she knows dem good, their leaders a nigga called Rogerton."

"I don't give a shit what his name is, gunshot don't respect names cuz."

"Feel you," Bonso laughs. "Hear me out nah, speaking to da dude an he was like ask your fams to run back da drugs and keep da jewels and money."

"Run back what fams?" Blacka laughed. "Dat shits turning over on da streets right as we speak. True it's not your ting or I would have run it on you cuz, got my little soldiers moving dat."

"I was like, man can't talk to him, nigga's a big man. Rogerton was like when we buck him, whateva innit. I jus laughed at him; swear down man laughed at him on da phone. One of my dargz sees Rogerton and a couple of dem in town, walking through Bricky and they were speaking to him. Blatantly he told dem da same ting, your link innit, man can't control you. If they want beef wid you then do your ting. He told dem straight tho, you don't carry it for show."

"Why you neva tell me blud."

"Dats soft cuz, dem men are half hearted crooks who know how to make paper. Don't get me wrong, they'll buss it, they ain't pussy, but they ain't ready for war wid yu fams, worst they know your famo. Fuck dat, it's all out steel innit. Novemeber the 5th will come quick if dem man try anything blud, fireworks day will greet their crew you feel me." Blacka laughed. "Yo cuz, what you doing weekend, come cross da waters fams, da man dem are going clubbing. Long time you don't rave over da dirty South."

"For real."

"Dis club blud, bare gyal, gyal like dirt blud trust."

"Yo, Bonso fuck tryin to get me to rave nigga. You comin for dis ting or what?"

"I'll send one of da gyal dem for it. You know niggas ain't movin like dat no more cuz."

"Who you sending?"

"Why?" Bonso asked.

"Who you sending?"

"Who do you what me to send?"

They both laughed.

"Dat link you hooked me up wid last time, tell her to drive and pick it up."

"I've got a different link for you," Bonso laughed. "Jus make sure she's back tomorrow wid my shit. She's coolie blud, real Indian, mum's got da red dot and all dat, yo cuz she love cock."

"Say no more, send her."

"Hold on, stay on da line fams, gonna call her now." Blacka sat there smoking and nodding to the music as he listened to his cousin on the other line. "She's coming to you now cuz. First the bitch was like I'm in bed got a headache, when I told her it's you she was like okay I'll do it. She wants to eat your dick off nigga."

Blacka laughed before asking, "Do I know her?"

"You ain't gonna member her, but she members you tho."

I listened as they spoke about another naive young female caught in the hype, doing all the wrong things, sex, drugs, guns and gangs, when would they ever learn; such a lethal combination. However, I enjoyed watching Blacka fuck these hoes, they could have his dick, but Blacka's heart belonged to me.

"Why, where have I seen her?"

"Blue's party, outside my yard, blud you're not gonna member her, but when you see her you're be like ah it's her."

"She's on her way."

"Yeah she's coming."

"Bitch better fresh and shit."

"You're fucked." Blacka laughed. "So what's da damage, how much should I give her for you?"

"Cuz do yuh ting, no rush, jus deal wid it innit."

"Bless cuz."

"Say no more."

"Member send da gyal back tomorrow."

"Shit you're gwanin like I'm gonna kidnap da bitch. What, her pussy dat good?"

They both laughed.

"Some hoes got better pussy than some gyal man call wifey, better believe cuz."

"You fuck these so called wifey's innit?"

"Yeah."

"Dats no wifey, they're undercover slappers' blud," they both laughed. "They're hoes blud, takin man for punk, dem gyal fi get dick slap. They're the worst cuz. Gyal wah gwan like their hearts genuine, dem gyal deh ave some hidden agenda blud."

"What you sayin some Star Wars gyal, heart dark like Vader."

They both laughed again.

"Yo cuz I'm gonna dash still, I'll give her da ting for you, and you'll see da bitch first ting in da mornin."

"Dat means late afternoon."

"Whateva."

The line went dead. Blacka threw the phone on the bed, and then lit up his zoot. He took a pull and then got up and opened his chest of draws. Moving his clothes around, he found what he was looking for. He smiled as he took out two condoms. Blacka sat back down and thought about the night ahead.

Weekend had come and Blacka decided to rave across the waters with his cousin and friends. Liquor filled the table in the V.I.P area where they sat and as normal, ladies flocked the very popular crew. For hours they sat there talking and entertaining the women with the odd occasional dance or two and the giving away of free liquor.

"Yo fams soon come?" Blacka said as he got up. "Cha Chu, mind your foot blud."

"Where you going fams?" Bonso asked.

"What you ducking out already blud?" Cha Chu added.

"Back in a minute, soon come." Blacka needed to piss and decided to head to the toilets. On his way there he saw three young ladies sitting at a table by themselves. As he stared at them, one of them felt his stare and returned the gaze. Her eyes followed him. They stared at one another, which now caused her friends to also look. One of them said something to the one whose attention he had originally caught, which made them all laugh. Blacka turned his head and kept walking. On his way back to his table their eyes made contact again, she smiled, Blacka returned the smile and kept it moving. As Blacka reached his table he asked his cousin and a few of the guys if they knew any of the ladies on that table. Bonso and a few of the guys had a look, neither of them knew any of the ladies at the table which Blacka was curious about, nor did any of the woman who had joined them in the V.I.P section.

Their response pleased Blacka. He was now determined to get to know her. He wanted something fresh, he knew he could have had any of the ladies amongst his friends, but he had now set his eyes on someone new. He had ordered a bottle of champs and sent it over to her table with a message specifically for her. To his surprise the bottle was returned.

His friends laughed. It angered him, he felt disrespected by the ladies especially her, but Blacka contained himself as he thought about what the bar staff had told him. She had said thanks but no thanks we're fine, and that she and her friends appreciate the kind gesture. Blacka recalled her words in his mind and decided to go over there to bring the bottle himself.

"Hi may I?" he said as he stood in front of her.

Her friend gestured for him to sit. Blacka sat down put the bottle on the table and introduced himself, they did likewise. The woman with whom Blacka's eyes were unable to depart from introduced herself as Mya, he introduced himself self using his real name Derrick. Conversation began flowing; laughter and humour filled the table. They had offered Blacka a glass of the wine from one of the bottles they had, and he accepted. Together they sat there drinking and talking. Blacka had not mentioned anything about the champagne. Everything had a time and a place, and he had no intention of breaking the vibes. Blacka had helped them finish both their bottles of wine, when one of the friends ordered another bottle.

"I'll pour it if you don't mind."

"You're a gentleman," said one of the friends.

"I try to be," he responded with a smile, and then looked at Mya who smiled.

Blacka licked his lips and then poured wine into everyone's glasses before pouring into his own. The timing was perfect. "I do apologise for sending the bottle of champs over here, I see you're independent ladies, I meant no disrespect, but dis beautiful lady captured my eyes, I jus wanted to do something nice."

"Aww, isn't he sweet," the friend looked at Mya. "I want some more ice."

"I'll go," said the other friend.

"Please, allow me. Do you ladies mind if Mya follows me to the bar, I promise to bring her back soon?" He smiled and put his hand up, "Promise, scouts honour." They both smiled at his humour. Blacka turned to Mya. "Mya, do you mind following me?

"Don't take long; remember we're waiting for ice."

"Promise, bring her back in a minute."

At the bar Blacka had charmed Mya even more, they exchanged numbers and both expressed their desire to meet up again, but in less noisy surroundings. Blacka accompanied Mya back to her table, gave her friends the ice, and offered them the champagne. He had told them it's the least he could do after drinking off all their wine, and thanked them for their company, which caused them to smile. Feeling now comfortable with him they accepted the bottle of champagne. As he walked off, he looked back and winked at Mya who smiled. He then turned around and walked towards the V.I.P section.

Blacka spent less than an hour with his cousin and friends when he decided it was time to leave, he felt hungry and tired.

Blacka jumped in his whip and drove down the road to the chicken shop, unable to find parking on the main; he parked on a back street and walked round. As he returned to his car he stood their munching on a fillet burger, when two dudes approached him.

"Where you from cuz?"

Blacka bit into his burger.

"Where you from?" the other guy asked. "Your face look familiar."

"Not from these ends, so now you're thinking to move to me yeah?"

Before they could say another word Blacka pulled me out, nervously they stared at me in fear. I was inching to attack. "Put your hands in the air, and get on your fuckin knees." Both men raised their hands and went down on their knees. "Don't fuckin move."

Blacka took knives out from both of their waists. "Rah, kitchen knives, you niggas ain't playin, you were looking to butcha sumting tonight to bloodclaat, an you chose me? He bit his lip. "Wrong choice nigga."

Let me at them, I wanted blood. Thoughts of going off crossed my mind, but then he wouldn't be doing my evil deeds and I wouldn't be living up to the purpose of my existence. I was made to serve man, over the years the leaders had found better purpose for my existence, they let me go into today's society especially the black community to encourage them to kill themselves with little influence.

"We weren't gonna do you nuttin cuz, you're on our ends innit, we jus wanted to know who you were."

"Fair play." Blacka ate the last piece of his burger. "Fuckin burgers cold man." Brap Brap, without warning he executed both men at point blank range. Blacka picked up the shells jumped in his car, not looking to bring heat to himself he took the back streets, and made his way back to West London.

Chapter 5

Cannot serve 2 masters

The following day Blacka lay on his bed as he listened to Mya telling him a bit more about herself, her family, her goals and aims in life. It was their first true conversation without the disturbance of music and friends; it was the perfect time for the exchanging words, a moment of communication, a moment in Blacka's life where a female's views and beliefs seem to have captured him in a web of passion. There was something about her he told himself, she was special he believed.

"You know I love the way you talk, I know I said it to you yesterday but you sound so sweet, it's actually cute."

"Thanks."

"For what?"

"Da compliment innit."

"So you like compliments ah?"

"Which woman doesn't?"

"You'll be surprised."

"Not being mean, but if you know women who don't like or appreciate compliments den there's something wrong wid dem, and you should have asked yourself, or better her about her past life. I guarantee you there's a connection. There are a lot of damaged goods out there, and I'm not jus referring to us women, you have a lot of damaged men out there too."

"Damaged in what way?"

"Emotionally, jus like how a lot of women are scarred from relationships, and childhood, you have brothas who are scarred from childhood too, no dad around, psychologically feeling neglected, yet physically don't understand why they're so bitter or confused, which can then affect how they treat women. You got the system affecting our people, especially the young black male who is supposed to be the stronghold for us women, and if brothas aren't playin or aren't able to play their role as provider, bread winner, strong positive role model because the system is set for them to fail, then yeah its natural they're gonna look elsewhere for their income, and once they turn to the streets they've fallen into the trap. Den comes death and incarceration, and den who's there to fend for the black woman?"

"I hear you."

"Dats the problem we're too busy hearin and knowin but not tryin to do anythin about it. Not being rude when I say dat."

"Cool, I feel you still." Blacka replied calmly.

"Trust me, us sistas got our issues believe, many sistas are getting it twisted and thinkin if my man can't provide for me den I'll look someone who can, or he's not ambitious enough, or I'm out shining him, when really we women have more options open to us in the system all attached with hidden agendas. The bigger picture is to destroy the black male, and as a people we become a rockin boat, and a boat dat rocks becomes unstable…you get me?"

"Dats deep still." Blacka added.

"Seriously, brothas need to do so much more to protect our women, but instead seem to be doing so much less. They've fallen straight into the trap. It's only natural if you make life harder for the black male; it makes it harder for him to provide for the black woman."

"You seem proper conscious."

"It's not even dat, I'm jus tryin to keep it real and don't get lost in da hype."

"For real."

"Our people are really messed up. We hate ourselves so much we kill ourselves."

"Why do you say dat?"

"Didn't you hear about the shootin which took place down the road from the club?"

"No. Why, what happen?"

Blacka caused my steel frame to become warm with laughter; he was a liar and a cold blooded deceiver. She wasn't just conversing with any murderer; she was speaking with the shooter himself, my prodigy. The name Blacka suited his dark side; he struck fear in the hearts of many, as old time Jamaican people would say beware of the blackheart man. With me in his hand, Blacka was undoubtedly a modern day boogie-man in the flesh, spilling blood and sacrificing mortality to fulfil my purpose.

"People were sayin two guys were shot in the head, and I guarantee it was black against black."

"Two guys for real?"

"Yeah, imagine operation trident had a field day. What other race has a task force assigned to dem, but blacks, and what makes it worse is dat we know we're being targeted, yet we're stupid enough not to realize it's time to set the wheel in motion and make a change. It's a joke."

"You're not jus educated, your street smart."

"Education will only get me the job I want, being street smart, as you call it, in my eyes it's being conscious of my surroundings and the choices I make. Being conscious of who I am, will not only help me survive in society, but keep me focused on where I'm going to; by remembering where we're coming from as a people. The past is the past, and it's called the past for a reason, but when you look how far our ancestors have come, surviving slavery, and then the long hard struggle to be free men and woman, for us today to turn around and be killin ourselves."

She sighed, before continuing to speak. "Our youths are being incarcerated for drugs and guns faster than they can supply dem on the streets, neither of which we have control over, it's not like we have the power to bring dem into the country on the large scale dat they exist, so who is? And to think it wasn't dat long ago that our ancestors fought for our freedom, and began liberating our minds, an all dis for what? For us to be actin like dis, joke, as a people we're really messed up."

Conversing with Mya seemed so much different from the usual women Blacka would talk to. It wasn't the fact that she was at university studying nursing; he had slept with many women who had finished or were attending university. To Blacka, university wasn't anything special; it was a commercially overhyped institute that no longer carried weight in the employment industry as it did back in the days. In Blacka's eyes to many people graduated from university unable to find a job and then had the burden of debt weighing on their shoulders.

Blacka lived the street life, and did what he wanted to do, nevertheless listening to Mya speak, had caught his attention, and it troubled me.

"It's true what you're sayin still, nuff youts are on da road ting, but most youts leave prison and turn Muslim which I think is a good thing."

"It is, least they find something, its better than returning to their previous lives. I bet you didn't know dat da white man wasn't the only people to enslave black people, the Arabs also enslaved our ancestors, before the white man."

"*For real*." Blacka sounded shocked.

"Yeah they enslaved black people. Would you believe me if I told you all the curses in the law of Moses dat the true biblical children of Israel were to face for the sins of their ancestors, points at us black people in the Western hemisphere. Member not every black person who came to the West were slaves, some were masters pets, you feel me."

"So you sayin the people of African descendent who went into slavery were black Jews?"

"On the real, the word Jew and everything based around it is an illusion. Put it this way, the word Jew refers to a descendent from the tribe of Judea, in Hebrew its Yehuda as there's no letter 'J' in Aramaic Hebrew. Therefore are they sayin every Jew in modern Israel, even more over the world are from the tribe of Judea, what about the other tribes and I'm sure they're not all blood descendents. Joke ting, the true Israelites went into slavery, and yes they were African descendents whose ancestors were black people from Mesopotamia."

"I don't know much about history, but I believe the Israelites of the bible were black. They were always going into Africa to escape and hide, you can't do dat if you're any other colour you feel me? Everyone knows da ancient Egyptians were black."

"Exactly, so back to slavery, who says they weren't in Africa at dat time and had moved further into the continent? Like you already know da real Egyptians were black, let me explain to you why I say the true Israelites are also black. The bible makes reference to dat wid da story of Joseph, are you familiar wid it?"

Listening to this Jezebel trying to seduce Blacka irritated me, her foolish words of wisdom and useless words of understanding meant nothing to the person I had created, her biblical philosophical doctrine of consciousness will never bring Blacka's heart from the darkness into the light.

"Nah."

"He was one of the twelve sons of the patriot Jacob, his brothas sold him into slavery in Egypt, anyway, during famine in their land his brothas went to Egypt to source food, he recognised them, but they didn't recognise him because he was dressed in Egyptian garments and in the position of ruler under Pharaoh himself, but the point I'm making is if he wasn't dark skinned like the ancient Egyptians den they would have noticed it was their brotha, but he fitted in and didn't stand out like a sore thumb."

"Dats deep. You proper know the bible an dat. I never did ask you what made you decide to leave Birmingham and study in London."

"No you didn't, and you never answered me when I asked you what you do for a living neither. The table on which you and your associates sat seemed very popular with the ladies, I wonder, was anyone entertainers, super stars or jus street men. So what do you do?

Blacka paused for a second as his mind quickly contemplated thoughts, as he weighed up his options. His spirit took to Mya and didn't want to lie to her, yet he couldn't bring himself to tell her the truth.

"I hustle green, I know it's not the best of lives but I'd rather sell the green than the white ting, no excuses but it's hard out here trust Mya, sistas are getting jobs easier than brothas."

"Yeah but dats a strategy innit, a working class woman not clued up every day comes home to a man whose got nothin, earning less or out on the streets immediately starts thinkin I can do better, he's nothin, etc etc, take away a man's pride make him feel worthless, you feel me. If our people truly knew their past, then its capable to preserve the future, and we would start looking within ourselves as individuals, couples and communities to build and heal, not make excuses, blame the white man, but know dat nothin could of happened to us or can happen without Yahweh allowing it, and when we realize dat, we'll find the solution."

On Blacka's chests of draws I lay listening to this bitch rant on as if she was Queen of Sheba, entertaining King Solomon, who the fuck did she think he was. Blacka is a killer, a cold hearted murderer whose heart is as cold as the temperature of my steel when buried in a plastic bag out in the cold on a dark winter's night. Does she think she can win his heart, its mine; I will never give him up. A foundation built on lies will never stand for anything, as long as he refrains from telling her the truth, their tomorrow is doomed, and he will never confess. Just like Danger he has two personalities, and if he ever thinks to leave me, well, we will cross that hurdle if and when it comes.

Blacka and Mya continued to talk for a little while longer before the conversation came to an end. Blacka lay there in silence as his mind absorbed all that Mya and he had spoken.

Blacka opened his eyes and looked at his diamond watch and realised he had been sleeping for hours. Damn, he thought to himself, that conversation with Mya was deep; he had tried so hard to process everything it had knocked him out. It was early morning and he had no intention of leaving the house again, Blacka got undressed and jumped into bed.

For the next couple of days, Blacka constantly spoke with Mya, he was mentally stimulated by her, she captured him, and he enjoyed being attracted to a woman for more than what she physically had to offer.

It was late evening and Blacka had not too long come off the phone with Mya. As he sat there thinking about her sweet intellect, thoughts of food ran on his mind, he decided he wanted something to eat. Not in the frame of mind to drive, Blacka picked me up shoved me in his waist, throw his hoodie over his head and walked out of the door. Not in the mood to trek it to Harlesden high street for some West Indian food, he settled for some chicken and chips, although deep in his heart he desired jerk chicken and rice and peas. On his way to the chip shop Blacka spotted someone with whom he had issues. I got excited as his heart rate increased, Blacka was mine, and we were a team no woman was going to come between us.

As we approached the car Blacka lifted his head up, and pulled me out of his waist. He held me in his hand, he loved the very sound I made as I released my glory, shouting out at the top of my voice like Mohammed Ali I shook up the world. "What you sayin now?" Blacka asked as he pointed me at him.

The enemy turned his back to us and placed his hands over his head, as if that would help, oh he knew I was coming.

Entering his flesh I ripped into his back, breaking his rib as I entered through his side, through the flesh of his hand I travelled straight into the side of his head and bored into his skull. Blacka and I left him slumped over the wheel of his car, as we made our escape.

A few days later Blacka and I went to meet his Queen of Sheba, Miss 'Think-she-knows-it-all,' black conscious bitch at her apartment, which she shared with her friends. Blacka did me the unthinkable; when we had got there Blacka had left me hidden in the secret compartment of his car. He had left me alone for a bitch he had put a woman before me. Friday nights were always ours. I was hurt and felt left out.

The following night Dean, Shaggy, Blacka and I went clubbing. Being their usual selves they entertained the ladies drank and got up to mischief. It was early hours of the morning and they decided to leave the venue. Unlike other street men, they considered themselves wiser, and never chose to leave a dance with the crowd but always left an hour or two before the scheduled finishing time.

As we travelled towards where Shaggy had parked his car, Blacka felt to piss, and walked towards the curb.

"Where yu ah go?" asked Shaggy.

"Piss, too much fuckin liquor,"

"Drink too fuckin much," responded Shaggy.

Blacka turned and smiled before crossing the road. Shaggy and Dean continued to walk.

Blacka walked up the road on the opposite side from his friends who had continued to walk as he stopped and began to piss against a wall, at the same time a car door opened. Blacka turned to face the sound, which had caught his attention. Out from the driver's side stepped a huge muscular man, both his and Blacka's eyes made contact. As they stared at one another a lady opened the car door and stepped onto the pavement. Blacka smiled.

"Yo blud you can't find a better place to piss," said the man as he walked around to where his lady stood on the pavement near to Blacka. "You never see us in the car sitting down?" He kissed his teeth and then held his woman and walked off.

"What, what you say?" Blacka said as he walked up towards them.

"You deaf," the stranger replied, after turning round to face Blacka. "I said couldn't you have piss in a better place. You see me and my girl sitting in the fuckin car, we saw you, you crossed over onto our side of the road and then you decide to piss when you approached us, you couldn't wait until we got out of the car, pass or something."

"Wa gwaan." Said Shaggy as him and Dean approached them.

"Honey come on," said the woman.

"Yo cool let go of me," responded the stranger. "What, you lot gonna gang up on me? What?"

"Baby come," she said nervously.

"Yo eediat, listen to yuh gal an walk, yu feel say your big chest can help yu." Shaggy lifted his top. Man will dun yuh life out ere."

"What, why, why?" he replied.

"Gwan yuh yard man, fool," Dean responded. "Before man duppy you."

Blacka stood there staring at him; I nudged him to remind him of my presence, to remind him I was there always in assistance.

"I didn't mean anything by it; I was jus sayin you could have pissed elsewhere. No disrespect big man," said the stranger.

"No disrespect." Blacka went silent for a second, as he bit his lip. "Bless. Cool," he said. Suddenly my cold frame became warm, I felt an instant rush of blood surface to Blacka's skin, his body became hot, and without another word he drew for me. The stranger stood there shook, trembling as I stared at him ferociously. Blacka again bit his lip.

"Please, please, don't kill me." He begged. "I'm sorry if I offended you, please don't kill me, please."

Blacka stood there for about fifteen seconds. "Alright cool." Blacka lowered me, yet his pulse raced, adrenaline pumping in his veins. I have grown to know Blacka, I fashioned him in my image, his heart it was as cold as me. The stranger turned to walk off. In a calm voice Blacka spoke. "Blud." He turned, instantly Blacka raised me at the same time closed his dominant eye which he used as a marker for accuracy. He pointed me, his trigger finger gave testimony to his heart and I spat at the stranger mercilessly, piercing his skin, ripping into his flesh and cracking his bone. Unfortunately for him my glory entered his temple, and lodged in his cranium. His lifeless body fell to the floor, blood flowed from the wound. If not wiped up by the police, the ants and flies would have a field day as this humid summer night would soon turn to daylight.

The girl screamed.

"Shut your fuckin mouth bitch before I silence it for you, shut up," said Dean. "And gi mi your bag."

She fell to the floor, tears poured from her eyes accompanied by her heavy breathing as she held her partner's lifeless body.

Blacka bent down and picked up the shell.

"You saw nothin bitch, open your fuckin mouth and your dead." Dean showed her driving licence to her. "We're keepin dis."

Dean and Shaggy ran off. Blacka shoved my shell in his pocket, and me he shoved in the front of his pants; this was my place of comfort. Blacka pulled his top down over me, and together we left the scene and caught up to the others. On the way home he had disposed of the shell in the canal. We made a great team Blacka and I.

The following day Blacka and I travelled down to South Kilburn estate. I listened as Shaggy and Blacka spoke about me as they sat down and smoked their weed.

"Shotta, you fi leggo dat now, dat bloodclaat hot like flames. Dat deh gun a walkin sentence blud. " Blacka smiled. "No joke ting my yout, fi real dat a life sentence."

Blacka leaned back in da sofa and pulled me out, then sat forward again. "Dis." He turned me back and forth. "My baby dis blud, yuh mad."

"Mad, a fuckin sentence dat."

Blacka laughed.

"Yu laugh." Shaggy smiled and shook his head at the same time. "Bloodclaat, Danger an I created a fuckin monster to raasclaat. Yuh a mad man u kno dat don't?" they both laughed. "Listen Blacka, melt da gun down, da gun too hot, too much man dead by it, plus it wanted in connection wid the murda over East."

"Bwoy, Shaggy blud, dis fuckin gun belonged to Danger. Dis is my lucky baby, dis was Dangers bruv."

"Yu get back Dangers jewellery don't?

"Yeah."

"Den no betta ting fi remind di I ah Danger den a bloodclaat gun."

I listened as Shaggy instigated to have me disintegrated, he wanted me gone. There was truth to his words, which made me uncomfortable. I waited for Blacka to point me in his direction, that I take the liberty and allow myself to go off, and silence Shaggy once and for all. History was repeating itself. He had bad mouthed me to Danger after a night of blood and violence, and was now doing the same to Blacka.

"Fams," Blacka explained. "Old gun new gun, five-O will give me life if they ever catch me on a murda anyway and if they stop me and I can't get away I ain't going in like dat famo, you mad blud. I ain't no half way criminal, mi and jail don't work blud. I couldn't last a fuckin day, fuck dat." Blacka laughed. "Fuckin wankin my life away behind bars, no pussy, rot in dat fucka blud." Blacka's facial expression changed, an evil smile cleaved to his face as he thought about all that he had done. Shaggy stared at him, awaiting Blacka to break the silence he had created. "Man dem are quick to buss it up on one anotha but fear pigs, fuck dat, they ain't takin me alive, it's a shootout blud." Said Blacka with a straight face.

"Oi, nah lie to yu blud, mi look inna yu eye an see a stone cold killa blud, mi fear fi yu, Jah kno." Shaggy smiled as he shook his head. "Danger and I create a monster to bloodclaat."

Chapter 6

Control

Night and day had passed and weeks had gone by, Blacka and I were inseparable, things were more or less back to normal. He had hardly spoken to Mya, I guess Queen of Sheba wasn't charming enough after all to capture King Blacka. The duo was back, her conscious interference had minimal effect, together we had robbed drug houses; car jacked fools for their chains, and shot niggas who tried to act brave. He was the trigger behind my wrath and I was the might behind his strength. You see, although these were Blacka's enemies, to me they were fuel to my fire. In the presence of mankind to promote wrath is my nature. What man has access to me, or any of my kind and thinks not to do harm? My sole existence is to do evil, create mischief of the heart and corrupt the mind. I had kept up my side of the bargain and as usual played my role whenever needed.

Blacka the lone ranger, NW10s very own Billy the kid was a dark force to reckon with, he had grown bold and strong in a system over clouded by illusions, which carried no wind. These clouds were here to stay and so was the black on black violence that tore through their communities like a tempest. My kind and I were flooded into their neighborhoods like great waters, washing them out and away slowly.

As I said before I am loyal to no man, the sole purpose of my creation was for destruction and to destroy. Even when I protect I destroy, to save a life, I have to take life. There is no justification or word to justify my purpose I'm a killing machine that is who I am, I'm a fuckin gun, and this is my nature.

Chapter 7

Eye opener

Jokes and laughter accompanied by the scent of high grade weed made its way out onto the streets as Blacka, Dean's uncle and a few of the younger's sat in Dean's bedroom. I listened as conversation turned from fun and jokes to the actions of the youth and how it impacted on their here and now, as well as future.

Dean's uncle had changed the conversation. It wasn't hard to tell when he spoke, people listened, he possessed an aura that commanded respect. He was an extremely older man for both Blacka and Dean, not to mention the two youths who were well known heads in their generation of up and coming thugs on the block, but he looked overwhelmingly good for his age.

Dean's uncle had done time back in the early 80s for shooting with intent and armed robbery. In the late 90s he was instigated, arrested and charged on a double homicide, and was found not guilty on both accounts.

His reputation back in the days for violence and no nonsense personality spread far and wide beyond the boundaries of North West London. In many people's eyes he was considered a people person and a community leader in spite of his violence. Dean's uncle had not too long been released from prison where he spent time on remand; in fact he was released just over a year ago, February 2011. He had made his usual travel to the States to see family and friends and business associates and was arrested and charged for a firearm he swears even up to today was planted by the police.

On more than one occasion I had heard Dean talk about his uncle being a bit of a black revolutionary back in the day. He had said he had brought that revolutionary spirit with him from the United States, where he resided a while after leaving Jamaica as a youth before migrating to England.

Blacka, Dean and many others on the block loved when he visited the hood, he would tell them stories of his life in the US, about Harlem and LA, and his connection with black organisations such as the Panthers. I had been there on one occasion with Danger and listened to this infamous black Robin Hood, talking about taking from the rich and giving to the poor, and the importance of community organisation and black awareness and empowerment. I must admit Dean's uncle sure did look in great shape for his age, and I guess his flash car and lavish lifestyle was appealing. To me he was just another nigga with money who once relied on the strength of my kind, he knew the power of the gun, yet I can't deny I found his pride and love for his people quite disturbing.

"You youts nowadays are fuckin crazy, I'm mean there's no structure in your shit. You make money all you do is floss, buy shit and make the system rich. How many of you invest in your community, do anything in your community?"

"Invest in da community," said Blacka. He looked at Dean. "I invest in those who invest in me."

"Dats the thing, we're lookin out for those who look out for us, and I feel you on dat; but me, when I was doing shit and even now dat I ain't doing shit, I still openly invest in my people. You see dat case I had in the States, you know who fought my corner every step of the way, was a guy from my old hood in Brooklyn, someone who a few of us invested in, he wasn't down for the streets, but he was down for the cause. Dis brotha didn't have heart to go out and take want he wanted, he wasn't about crime, this brotha was about education; so we paid dis young bluds tuition fees to law school, we provided him with the utmost support every step of the way, and don't get it twisted, we didn't do it so dat when situations like dat shit dat caught me in States arrive we can call upon a brotha, nah, we did it to empower. Do you know what he's doing now?" In silence they listened, he had totally captured their attention. "On weekends he's educatin our young brothas and sistas about law, while at the same time paying for anotha brotha at university studyin engineering. You see dis is a movement of love, self love. You need to stop thinking like niggas and think like men. It ain't about being down for the hood, it's about raising your people. And we ain't jus investing in America, we have schools in Africa, land and agriculture going on, brothas and sistas in education, studyin law, medicine, plumbing, electricial engineering, all different fields and as one begins to strive the key is to pull someone else up with you, feel mi young blud, dats how were doing it over Africa."

"Rah, man neva look on it like dat still, if man dem aren't down for the ends, den man ain't shit innit, but listening to you still, dats deep. Man all rob and intimidate those youts, try and convert dem and dat, nah lie, all take dem for eediat. When really they're in the struggle jus like man, but chose a different path to fight it on," said one of the youths.

"For real," said the other youth.

"Uncle true we don't have no structure like you lot, back in those day you had loads of black organisations on the rise, we don't have dat no more, not like how you had it."

"What you talkin about, you have more organisations today than we ever had, and it's not about the organisations out there, it's about da organisation you have in you," he pointed to Dean. "And you," he pointed to Blacka and you and you." He pointed to the two youths. "The foundation of an organisation must begin from within for it never to be destroyed. Let's take it back beyond Black panthers, we all know bout Marcus Garvey right. Well Garveyism isn't dead, every time you see a brotha or sista speakin bout unity, community, you hear the spirit of the honourable Marcus Garvey speakin through dem, and Garvey he got his spirit from someone before him, you feel me. Dis is an endless cry of ancestral spirits cryin out whether our leader's messages were the same or not, the spirit and intention had only one objective and dat was to build, build and build community. Love one anotha young blud's."

"Shits fucked up now though we can't even go up the road without beef," said one of the youts.

Blacka laughed. "Your generation are fucked, at least we, our generation link up wid man dem from all bout, you fuckas don't leave your ends, all dis neighborhood bullshit. Dis tension in North West wasn't the same as it is today. Areas at war were more or less one syndicate, and the funny thing is dis is happenin everywhere."

"Glad you see it Blacka. It's happenin everywhere, all over England, it's a strategy they've been using in the States for a good while now to keep the youts on tight lock down. The world is not much different from a prison. Jamaica same thing, areas in Jam Down where there was one area don, they now have numerous little communities and multiple dons and gangs, the smaller your circumference the tighter your movement, the less you know or even think about what's going on around you."

"Dats deep," said the yout.

"Think outside the box, they say you see more when you're outside the box then when you're within it, step out young blud, step out dat shit."

His words to me bared no substance; the system that created me always had a way of tearing black people apart. Divide and conqueror, it was a proven method never to fail, as long as the black male continues to think like a nigga.

Whenever black people show any sign of togetherness, integration, and community, there is always an operation in line to physically and mentally control them, whether it's through the media, educational system, or opportunity disadvantages, the system will destroy their pride, and give them in return drugs, and guns, a harlot for a son and a prostitute for a daughter. Dividing the masses has never failed.

"Elder your wise still," said Blacka.

Personally I thought he was an ego tripping nigga who had once rapped his fingers around the cold steel of many of my ancestors, and had used us to kill the ancestors of those he now preached to, damn hypocrite.

"Let me tell you something young blud, I neva robbed my own people, we had pride. I wouldn't stand there and say I haven't killed my own, I have, but when one of your own is willing to turn informant or try to bring down what you all tryin to build and breaks da code and does harm to his own black brotha or sista, den he ain't a brotha no more. You feel me; dats black pride. Back in our time we robbed corporations, organisations, and businesses, we weren't robbin one anotha on the block," he shook his head. "Shits fucked up. You young brothas need to think outside dat physiological, sociological and psychological box. You don't go places like Muswell Hill and see liquor stores and betting shops on every fuckin block and corner. Open your eyes young blud."

I was in a place where I wanted to be not, as I had no option but to listen as he spoke more about coming together, investing in the youth. He used the British army as example, and the principle of the various roles people play to make it a success. The principle behind his example was that not everyone needs to be out on the field, attacking the battle head on, some are better neutralised in other areas of expertise. From beneath Blacka's garments I felt a feeling of discomfort, his breathing was too steady, he was too relaxed, the atmosphere was too peaceful; who the hell did Dean's uncle think he was Mr Black almighty.

Later that evening Blacka had phoned his Queen of Sheba, he had apologised for not being in touch of late, and had promised to make it up to her. I felt disheartened, betrayed and was upset. Mr Black almighty and Miss Queen of Sheba were polluting Blacka's mind. Blacka was a killer, he delighted in death, he loved the streets, we had made thousands together, he had a comfortable lifestyle because of our partnership, and now she wanted to take him away from me. Blacka had promise to make it up to her by visiting her that very night, he had picked her up and took her to a hotel, again he had left me in his secret compartment.

The following evening he had visited her again, but this time he stayed over at her place, I guess he thought he'd make it up to me by carrying me into the house.

He did likewise for weeks, and I began to contemplate our agreement. He showed the streets no love, instead he sponsored the local football team and gave them money to buy new kits and balls, and encouraged the youths to never give up on their dreams. He was going through a phase, one that disturbed me. Dean's uncle and this black so called Hebrewess were corrupting his mind with ambitious thoughts about the dream of a better tomorrow.

Blacka had shared with her more of his life on the streets but kept us a secret and me out of her sight. Night after night I listened as Samson gave his strength to Delilah. I couldn't bear listening to her encouraging him he could do better, what does she know? Has she seen him in his sore displeasure, does she know his anger, his bitterness. I wanted him to see her as Delilah, someone who would betray him, but instead she made him strong, and I felt betrayed.

Whenever his associates called to get together, my spring rejoiced and my hammer was ready to give shout, we were on the go, but not this time. Blacka, Dean and a few others sat around a table and were talking about investing as if they were a cooperation, or the Knights of the Round Table. Our only investment was in guns and drugs to sell, everything else was crack dreams.

One month later

Blacka's phase bothered me, and my spirit really kindled against him when he accepted to move in with her. The thought of Blacka, her and I sharing an apartment wasn't a part of the agenda, neither was it tolerable. She had told him they could rent a place near her university; go halves on the rent, and if he agreed it would not only show her how he felt about her, but it would get him away from the ends and streets. I really can't believe he accepted. Blacka had visited her at her home that evening. She had cooked him a meal and later they made love in a way which was passionate beyond measure, I felt troubled. The thrill I give Blacka when I bark after the enemy stimulates him, its undeniable Blacka is aroused by me, but what I witnessed if truly he really opens his eyes he'll know I could never satisfy him like that and it frightened me. At that moment I wished she would pick me up and hold me in her hands so that I could let myself go off and eliminate this future problematic situation.

The following night it felt great to be in Blacka's room, on the ends and away from her influential black consciousness. He had spent the day on the block, with Shaggy, Dean and a few more of the goons. I was a bit disheartened to hear them agree with her that moving out the ends was a good thing. Blacka was known, had enemies and didn't give a damn, neither did any of the others, and all of a sudden Dean's uncle and Mrs Queen of Sheba come into Blacka's life and cold hearted niggas who had balls of steel turn pussy. Grow a pair I thought; as I listened to them speak from beneath Blacka's garments. Should I let myself off I considered, right here and now, give them a wake-up call, and remind them of the testimony of my strength and my capability to do damage, my sole purpose and why they all fell in love with me and others of my kind. But I had faith in Blacka to come around out from his trance and take what he wanted as we used to do.

Blacka had told Dean and Shaggy to continue to let the goons turn the money over, and do what they needed to do. He planned to lay low for a bit and chill out.

Chapter 8

Draw out

Two days later my wish came true, we were out there rolling and I was excited. Dean had gone to pick up some money and was shot at by some youths in an area they had set up shop. Blacka had grabbed me and left Mya instantly, it seemed Mrs Queen of Sheba's wisdom wasn't wise enough to keep Blacka from his boys. There was hope for us after all, even if I couldn't keep Blacka on the streets, as long as he connected with his boys and they were, he would be loyal to the streets through his boys.

That day we had brought fear to that neighbourhood gang. We had not only spilled blood during the day, but early morning after the police had left the scene and the tape which they had put was up removed, we had revisited the area kicked off a door and did what we do best.

Chapter 9

Disconnected

Two weeks had passed and Blacka and Mya were now living like husband and wife in a two bedroom house with an en-suite bathroom, and it sickened me. I was no longer in control, in fact I no longer felt a part of his life. Blacka had shut me away in the darkness; he had wrapped me up in a plastic bag removed the white bath panel, placed me under the tub, replaced the bath panel and screwed the screws back in.

Night and day they tormented me with words of love for one another, big dreams and future plans. Blacka had invited his sister and nephew up to the house. Cassandra had loved her for her positive influence on her brother, as for Melekiah, well; he was just a little boy, as long as you played with him, he would love anyone.

That night after Cassandra and his nephew had gone home, I listened as he told her about Danger, what kind of guy he was and the family life he desired, which was cut short, due to the street life. He had told her about his death, which caused him to cry.

Mya had never seen him like this, and when asked what he did about it he went silent. She must of had held him in her arms as I heard her say come. She had asked him again, his reply was, have you ever lost someone so close to you. He had just shot himself; he might as well have confessed. By her reaction, she now knew he was more than a drug seller, he was a killer too. I no longer heard Blacka's voice and assumed he fell asleep, I hoped it would be a wakeup call for both Blacka and Mya, they were two different individuals, on the search for two complete different goals. Now she knew the real Blacka, who was a cold blooded killer, Miss self righteous Queen of Sheba would walk, departing from this relationship and go her separate way, which would then allow me and Blacka to live our lives the way we know best.

To my surprise days went by, a week followed, and a month pursued and the sound of their relationship only seemed to get stronger. Mya encouraged Blacka and continued to speak to him about history, culture, love and development. She saw something in Blacka I now saw, or rather wished not to see. Blacka was getting smart and if it's one thing I hate, it's a self-educated black male, but love myself a nigga. Jealousy and rage tormented me. I was never created to love, neither could I love, yet here I listened to two people displaying affection so warm and conversations so heartfelt, it frustrated me, and I began to question myself.

Am I really just another twisted symbolical version of the erected penis when looked upon from a side view? Is there nothing more than negativity to my existence? I wanted answers. Dr Frances Cress Welsing seems to think so; I heard Mya read it to Blacka from her book the Isis Papers. The penis produces life, I take life, is the function and appearance of my magazine and the handle it slides into the replica image of man's hanging testicles. Do I cock back like the uncircumcised? Why does Mya torment me with knowledge of this women and her crazy imagination, poisoning Blacka's mind against me and my kind.

A month had come and gone and I was still hidden away in darkness. Out of sight out of mind, Blacka no longer needed me. I had heard him speak with Dean and Shaggy over the phone, as they brought him up to speed, about their investments both legal and illegal. They planned to turn their business around completely and go hundred percent legit. They had planned to invest in the Caribbean and in Africa, but needed to make a trip to the great African continent to see for themselves where and what they could do.

Blacka's associates had visited him a few times and Mya had preached the gospel to them. The funny thing is they had admired her and on numerous times they had told Blacka she was good for him. They were wrong, I was good for him, have they forgotten without me and my kind they would never have risen to power.

Blacka had told them of his trip he planned with Mya to the part of the African continent now called the Middle East once she graduates from university and depending on the outcome; he'll know where his future lies, but the team investment was crucial and a priority at the moment so they would have to fly out and get a feel of the place.

Blacka had hooked Bonso up with a tight contact, which gave him high grade on consignment and in large amounts, as well as arms if needed. Things were moving fast.

I was more than outraged and confused as I listened to him speak as if he had power and street credit without me. I gave him his respect on the streets, without me he was just another feeble mortal, someone whose very nature resembled my creator. What do humans know about love, I was created to destroy?

Father why did you create me, why did you let me go into the black community? When all I do is get abused by these so called thugs who scream death to you all. If they really respected my power would they treat me this way? No one loves me, not even you father. No one loves me. I'm abused and used, ill treated and left hidden away in all manner of dark, dirty, dusty, cold and wet places, you send me and my kind into their communities, is it not natural if they do thy will, shall we not grow attached? I am hurt, betrayed, he loves me no more, and neither will he do your dirty work. Where does that leave us?

I hated Blacka with a passion, I wanted him gone. My wrath had kindled for him; I wanted to burn his skin. I wanted him to feel what he felt when he faithfully loved me, during our reign of terror. He had forgotten our blood covenant, and the oath of togetherness.

If he had not taken the magazine out, plus the one in the head, I would have set myself off, to remind him of my power and presence. But he had, and then it clicked to me, Blacka had not totally forgotten me, if he had he would of gotten rid of me as Shaggy told him to, Blacka still needed me, he just felt he would use me when he feels. Well, revenge is sweet. They say leave all vengeance to God, well I am my own God, and I shall have my vengeance one day. Blacka shall feel my wrath.

Chapter 10

Shits Never Forgotten

Month later

"Ghana was pretty yu fuck, it's like a big Jamaica, man neva wah leave, nah lie blud," said Shaggy.

"Were investing there blud, I want a house there, trust. Fuck England it's a shit hole." Dean responded. "You don't get value for money here, look dis place dat Blacka is renting, if da owners sell dis, you know how much hundreds of thousands for it, you can build a fuckin massive house in Africa for dat."

"England ah jus money man, once yu have it, leave it," replied Shaggy.

"Well dem Ghanian's are sayin they'll sort out the land and deeds. Let's buy acres, massive land divide it and every man build their house on it. Start a little community, feel me."

Listening to Blacka plan a future far away without me hurt, he had forgotten our covenant of blood, the sacrifice of flesh. The partnership of doom, we were a team, and undoubtedly he showed need for me no more. He was sincerely planning to end our oath, well over cold steel, and his dead body will we depart, mark my word.

"Mans been back here for two weeks now, and trust I don't even want to be here, it feels like I belong there blud." Dean stated.

"Dean, Africa awaits its creator," Shaggy replied. "Yo, mi nah lie still, dem deh ting wa Mya ah teach man bout di bible and black people inna di West, and di Holy Land, ah sum deep ting. Wa'appen if wa she ah seh real, an ah Palestine wi belong. Like how she seh a raiment of his people shall return, although they shall be like di sands of di seas in numbers scattered all over di world. Blessed are those whose names written in di book of life. Yu see di way she break it down still, Jah kno, bomboclaat, mi ah tell yu di gyal deh wise yu fuck."

"Mya's deep blud, she got me thinkin. What happens if we're really from dem lands and the white man tricking us to make us think were originally from West Africa? When you think about it, Africa is full of blacks, we were taken from Africa, so teaching us we come from there originally is more convincing, and less likely to seem suspicious, yo it deep blud. When you and Mya are going to the Holy Land, I'm coming blud trust, man wah see wah gwan for dem self. I'm taking my gyal too."

"For real Dean, mi waan see if my spirit connect blud, see mi ah seh. Cah mi no seh dem deh Jews an no Jews. So, who ah de real Jews or Israelites then? See when mi tell mi babymudda dem ting deh, true she a Christain an can relate to di bible, she seh Mya different, and dem ting deh deep, she seh she wa link up wid her. Mi ah tell wifie wi ah go ah Israel."

"As Mya pointed out, why would they rather be known as Jews and not Israelites. Yo blud dis is deep."

"Look at us jus sittin back and sippin on some juices and shit, dis is it bruv, dis is di life. A future wid no cops, no bullshit, jus conscious vibes, no negativity, fuckin England, England breeds dat negative shit like germs."

"England is cockroach, bare shit inna it," Shaggy responded.

They all laughed.

Blacka looked down at his mobile phone as it rang. "Hello," he said as he answered it. "What da fuck!" He shouted. "What da fuck you tellin me, dem pussies are dead. I'm gonna fuckin kill everyone of dem. I swear I'm gonna kill all of dem."

"Wa gwaan king?" asked Shaggy angrily. "Wa di fuck ah gwaan?"

"What's up fams." Dean asked looking angry yet confused.

"Nah, fuck," Blacka shouted.

"Gi mi da bloodclaat phone." Shaggy snatched the phone out of Blacka's hand. "Ah who dis, wha gwaan? Wha gwaan my yout?"

"Back in a minute," said Blacka. "Fuck dis, its war." As Blacka cursed I heard his voice getting louder and louder as he drew near. The bath panel was off. I felt his hands grip the plastic bag.

He entered back in the living room with me in his hands. So, he needed me now. He had just planned a future without me and now wanted team commitment, to walk in our covenant again, the same covenant in which he had broken. My hand was no longer stretched out, neither was my power with him. "They fuckin killed my cousin. We should have never underestimated dem pussies blud. Now my cousins dead and Bonso's in jail."

"Yo tek dis." Shaggy handed Blacka his phone. "My yout ah seh di pussy dem cut Bonso sista throat. Yu dun kno Bonso a hot head. Him and da man dem go look fi Rogerton dem and kill two ah dem in front of bare people. My yout seh when wi come him will tell wi everyting."

"So how Bonso reach jail blud?" asked Dean.

"Police kick off him gal door an find him wid gun. Him an him likkle right hand Cha Chu, da police dem hold don't. Yo, kill we fi kill da whole ah dem an cut left ya blud, run left England now."

"For real, leave a blood bath behind us." Dean responded.

"Yo fuck dat deh ting yu have inna yuh hand," said Shaggy as he looked at me. "Come wi go ah South and arm up wid some real artillery, and bun some bwoy skin."

"Fuck dat." Blacka shoved me in his pants. "Let's go."

Chapter 11

Judgement

In a house over South London they sat preparing themselves for war.
Bonso's friend had placed on the dining room table before he had left to return two Mac 11's, a Mac 10, two 357 magnum revolvers, a twelve gague pump action, an a mini Uzi.

"Take what you want," said Ticka as he entered the room. "Dis is me." He had in his hand two 9mms. "I don't know why da fuck he went back to his girls, and have their guns on dem, him and Cha Chu should have never gone there. After we bun da man dem and everyting in the house in broad daylight an bare people see what went down, they should have known the heat was on."

"So fams, what fuelled dem to get so brave?" Dean asked. "Cos Rogerton and his goons have seen Blacka, they saw him at the dance wid you man dem, and they've seen us more than once come link the man dem. So I don't get it, what they on drugs, niggas mus be on fuckin drugs?"

Ticka shook his head.

"Wah kind of mad move yu lot dun blud. In front of everyone, not even masked," Shaggy said.

"Blud man was masked, but they know it was us, the retaliation was too swift." Ticka explained. It wasn't jus about Blacka fam, they're carryin feelings about dat don't get it twisted, but it's not even dat blud, they violated big time, it was jus a reaction ting you feel me."

"How you mean," said Blacka in an angry voice. "Dem pussies fi get gunshot yes," he said as he reached into his pocket for his phone which had jus begun to ring.

"Wah kind of fuckery yu ah talk, some Billy the kid bullshit, and now di man dem lock up. Stop di fuckery, anger no mek it right now my yout, cut di bloodclaat fuck…"

Blacka interjected. "Man dem quite, Mya's on the phone." He answered. "Wa gwan babes, hold on a second, we're watching a movie at Price's house, let me leave the living room so they can un-mute the TV." He got up and headed out the room.

"Tell Mya hello," said Shaggy.

"Shaggy said hi." As he was about to exit the door, he turned back and smiled. "Mya said hi." Blacka walked into the kitchen. "What you up to babes?" he asked using a sweet tone.

How humans concealed their grief and clothed their anger only gave testimony to their cunning nature and deceitful ways. I listened as Blacka laughed, joked and charmed Mya with words, and not once did he mention the circumstance at hand. I guess he thought he was protecting her, but subconsciously was he really protecting himself, she had begun to rule him, he was no longer a cold blooded killer who desired street power and respect, he had grown weak, fallen to Delilah, a woman had taken his strength.

"So what time will you be home," Mya asked. "I know what it's like sometimes when you get together."

Blacka laughed. "Bout 12 or 1, don't wait up for me, but I'll wake you when I come."

"I bet you will."

"You know you're irresistible."

"I love you too."

Like this very system they lived in, their relationship was built on lies, and they've talked about the corruption that manifests in high and low places, do they not know their relationship shall fall likewise. Poor Mya all her conscious thoughts and speeches were all in vain.

Blacka re-entered the room, "Ticka, tell us the full hundred nah," he said as he sat back down.

I had listened as Ticka had explained everything leading up to the murder of Bonso's sister, and the swift revenge attack in details. He had told them that, Bonso, and Cha Chu had seen two of Rogerton's soldiers strolling on Acre Lane as they were walking to the West Indian restaurant. As the guys walked pass the shop they were staring hard. At that time Bonso clocked the play and went and stood next to the side wall facing the door and left Cha Chu in the queue. About ten, fifteen seconds later they entered the shop, and demanded to be served, at that time Cha Chu was ordering. Without hesitation Bonso punched one of them in his jaw and knocked him down and began stamping on him. Cha Chu had hospitalised his friend after repeatedly beating him with the butt of his gun, fracturing his cheek bone, occipital socket and also causing haemorrhage and tear of the eyeball due to direct contact from the edge of gun.

About an hour later Bonso had received a call from his sister who sounded distressed; in the background he could hear people shouting and had asked her what's up. Before she could answer Rogerton came on the phone, according to Ticka, he must have snatched it from her and began shouting threatening remarks to him down the phone. Ticka had told them he remembered Bonso saying come and collect my sister's body; pussy if you touch my sister I'll kill your whole family. Rogerton must of handed Bonso's sister the phone back, Bonso asked her where she was, as soon as she mentioned where; we hasted out the door. Bonso kept calling her name, Bonso heard her choking, and then all of a sudden she went silent, nothing but their voices he could hear until that too ceased to exist. By the time we reached at the spot, there she lay with the phone on the floor next to her in a pool of blood. One of them had slashed her throat; in the process her carotid artery was severed. She had lost so much blood; there was no chance of her surviving. They had killed her like a sacrificial animal.

Tooled up and armed for war they went looking for them and found some of them in a house on Stockwell Park Estate. Bonso had spread the word and had received information of their whereabouts through an individual who they gave weed on consignment to on a regular basis.

The informant was affiliated with the enemy, and wanted no part of the current situation. He had met up with Bonso and the others and told them where they were, believing that he was going to pick up two keys of high grade weed on consignment. The only thing he received was a one way ticket to hell. They had stabbed him multiple times and slashed his throat leaving him with his seat belt still around him; head slumped forward as he sat dead in the driver's seat of his car.

His own disloyalty caused his death. Selling out your own gang just to keep your drug link showed no loyalty, no real street principles. I have heard many stories over the years, and to me it seems there aren't many true street soldiers, if they aren't selling out one another over money, they're working with the police, some way or another.

Ticka had explained that they went in all guns blazing, as they kicked off the door to the lower ground apartment flat, as some entered through the door others opened fire through the window.

"Well you know what blud, I don't care about the yout who got shot in the kitchen, nida da mother, fuck dem all. It should have been me, I'd kill everyting in dat. Believe," said Blacka with a straight face. Fuckin kill my cousin, I'm pissed Bonso's in jail, but in the heat of the moment nigga would have done the same ting."

"I feel you," said Ticka. Frustrated he gripped his gun. "But now dada's gone. He's gonna get a fuckin bird blud, I aint worried bout anyone coming forward as witnesses, fuck dem man will duppy dat, dada and Cha Chu got caught with straps blud, dem straps murdered nigga's. Ticka shook his head. "Cha Chu shot the yout blud, he's fucked, can't believe man dem had the straps on dem."

"I'm fuckin killin everyone of dem tonight blud."

"Yeh man, dem man ah get coppa tonight," said Shaggy. He inhaled and exhaled a cloud of smoke in the air. "Ah di hot head ting, ah it fuck up gangsta still, mi ah vet inna this killin ting, an mi ah tell yu, Bonso mek ah wrong move, mi hear wha yuh ah seh Blacks, no mi feel yu Blacka, but emotions and revenge togedda no mek it, man can't link dem togedda, ah dat fuck up gangsta. Yu notice seh when Danger and I touch road everyting get fuck, we nah jus rush out pon bwoy an gwaan like ah Texas we deh, wi pick pussy like grape, plan an one one shot di pussy dem down."

"Yo fams I'm not sayin what the man dem did was smart, runnin out there an fuckin actin all crazy, fuck prison. I'm jus sayin I understand his reaction," said Blacka. Shaggy nodded as he puffed on his spliff. "Niggas gonna get these muddafucka's, pick dem off like grapes, I'm gonna fuckin peel niggas crown like banana blud."

"Dem bwoy a walkin dead." Shaggy added. "Dat mi kno."

Later that evening hidden behind black balaclavas they stormed into a house in Tulse Hill, separating the occupants within. The woman and her child were led at gunpoint into the bedroom and promised to remain unharmed as long as they kept quiet while the man remained in the living room with numerous guns pointing in his direction, one of which frightened him the most. Dean stood right in front of him, trembling he stared down the nozzle of a twelve gauge pump action.

"Pussy down pon yuh knees," Blacka said as he stepped closer pointing a 357 magnum at his chest cavity.

Dean thrust his shoulder forward, his arms closed the distance between him and the enemy, causing the front of the gauge to jam him in his face, catching him on the mouth, and busting his lip. "Open your mouth bitch," said Dean. "Wide muddafucka."

Blacka shoved the 357 revolver inside his mouth. "Gi da gun a blowjob pussy, suck pon di nozzle bwoy," said Shaggy. "Suck it like how yu suck yuh gal tinkin pussy."

On his knees he trembled as his lips compassed Blacka's strap.

"You like it innit," Blacka laughed. "Cock sucka."

"Blacka wha yu ah ramp wid di pussy for, buss it off in nah him face and ejaculate marrow my you….."

Before Shaggy could finish saying the word yout Blacka pulled the trigger. The impact from the shot sent his head backwards, flesh flew towards the wall staining the wallpaper, as blood decorated the wall, settee and laminated floor. His lifeless body fell towards the floor.

My anger kindled against Blacka even more, he had given my glory unto another, it should have been my kill.

"Movements," said Shaggy as he walked towards the living room door.

Blacka followed leaving a horrific sense of blood, flesh and scattered fragments of bone on the settee, and floor.

Chapter 12

Revenge

Later that night it was time to touch the road again. Tooled up and ready for war they got into two different cars from what they had used earlier. These were what they called working cars. They were motors purchased for purposes like these; log books were never changed and they remained hidden away from the public streets until moments like now. Using the information which they had previously gathered they went out in search of Rogerton and fellow members of his crew.

Things never go as planned and this was one of those moments.

"Dat was Rogerton blud." Ticka shouted.

"Where," Blacka responded, "Where?"

"Turn around, in dat fuckin car dat jus passed. He's got two goons in there wid him."

"An da man dem behind us no spot him nida, yu sure say ah him?" replied Shaggy as he pulled into a side road to turn around. The second car followed.

Blacka's phone rang. "Its Dean," said Blacka before answering. "Yo blud dat was Rogerton back there, fuckin niggas movin like man in an unknown car. Ticka spot him in da back seat."

"What da fuck mans waitin on let's do dis now blud. We were wondering why you turned around. Lets cap dis nigga now. He didn't see you."

"I don't think so; fuck it, I don't care if he did anyway. Were gonna pull up on those niggas. Yo, gone blud." Blacka ended the call, "Let's do dis blud."

Shaggy put the car in gear and drove back in the direction they were coming from. The second car followed.

What happened next wasn't what they expected, but then what is to be expected when dealing with the unexpected. Street war has no law to it but kill or be killed. Down the road at the traffic lights, the two cars waited one behind the other, wondering if they would catch up to Rogerton and his goons.

The hunters became the pray. Suddenly the sound of guns barking caused Shaggy to run a red light, before stopping in a safe place. Out the whip guns in hand they returned the fire.

Rogerton had seen them alright, and knew they spotted him also. He judged right, he believed they would turn around and pursue and so they did. Rogerton and friends had lay wait their arrival, and greeted them with gunfire.

Unfortunately time wasn't on the side of the driver of the second car and he was unable to move fast enough. The driver received a gunshot to his shoulder, instantly he braced back and turned his face away from the shooter as he drew for his strap and took a bullet to his neck, which flew through the soft tissue of his flesh boring through his Adams apple and out the other side and into Dean's upper arm. There was no hope for the driver, he was a gonna.

Pellets from the red cartridge which dropped to the floor of the car as Dean pulled the trigger shattered the back seat window on impact, hitting his target throwing him to the floor. Dean jumped out the whip, in his blood stained garment he opened fire again.

Blacka and Shaggy pinned one of Rogerton's foot soldiers behind a car and blazed it after him from two directions he had no where going. However, when fear and fright takes hold of man who knows the outcome. In his case, the outcome was death, inescapable. Foolishly he desired to run instead of taking cover and holding his ground; how amateur, as if there was any place to go, what about being pinned down didn't he understand.

Oh, I was driven to rage, Blacka's 357 magnum revolver roared like a mighty beast, shaking the night sky as it tore flesh, while shaggy's Mac 11 caused the rain to come as he showered him with bullets.

Rogerton's ambush wasn't going to plan, and myself, I wasn't getting any of the action. Blacka had given my love to another, he had disregarded our covenant, our oath to take life, destroy and commit sin was broken; he had favoured another. I was jealous, my jealousy raged hate within me.

Swiftly gun police swooped down and all hell broke loose. Blacka and team were no longer in conflict with just Rogerton, they were in direct conflict with feds too. If you ask me, in Rogerton's eyes they couldn't have come at a better time; he had just become a one man show with nowhere to run and out gunned. The situation was bad and it was time to get out of there, having a shoot out with police was the last thing anyone wanted. Well, at least I would have thought so.

Ticka surprised me, 9mm's in both hands he confronted the police, which caused the others to do so likewise. The odd few people who were on the streets at that time had long dispersed out of sight, leaving what would be considered something out of a movie scene on the streets of London. For those who watched from a distance, were ever so far, yet so close. For them, it was a bit like watching Boyz in the Hood or Menace II Society, but in 3D.

This movie lacked a star, get rid of that revolver, and return to your first love. Let's give them a show they will never forget. But Blacka refused to remain faithful, I watched as he reloaded and reloaded.

By this time Shaggy had cut and made a run for it, after seeing armed police gun down Ticka. I must say, Ticka went out like an action hero; two guns in hand blazing like Billy the kid.

I know not what became of Dean as Blacka took me on a quest. He had seen Rogerton slip away from the scene, and no way did he intend to let him slid. Keeping low and out of sight we slowly gave chase and followed him into the nearby housing estate. Blacka checked the 357-magnum revolver and realized he only had two shots left. Although he wore gloves, he cleaned it nevertheless, before placing it on the floor under a car and pulled me out.

My chamber inhaled the fresh air as he held me, gripping me tightly in his hand. I felt free. Man I knew at that point what it felt like to be free from prison, what it felt like to be incarcerated bound to life without action. Longing to participate in an activity that stimulates ones nature, yet unable, due to restrictions and restraints, oh yes I felt bitter. He released me; and now what does he want me to do, be faithful, keep the law, or covenant.

On a dark quite street on the housing estate Rogerton stood facing the opposite direction with his back to us, with panic in his voice he spoke on his mobile phone.

Blacka's blood pumped heavily through the pulse of his finger. Kindled with anger towards him, yet I felt aroused. I remembered the good times and this warm sensational feeling as his fingers pulsated against my steel. I wanted to forgive him for all his sins against me; I wanted to kill for him, to take life at his command, to rip his enemies flesh from their bone and spill their blood as a sacrificial offering.

"Pussy don't move," Blacka rushed at him and butt him in his face. As he went down Blacka pointed me at his chest, and began to frisk him. Disarming him of his strap, Blacka shoved it down the back of his pants. Blacka stepped on his mobile phone crushing it under his foot. "Pussy on your knees, now."

"Yo blud, please don't kill me."

Blacka raised his hand, coming down at an angle he bitch slapped him with the side of the gun. "Shut your fuckin mout. You killed my cuz, my fams going prison; nigga you fuckin on drugs? My niggas maybe dead right about fuckin now. In shoot outs with five-O, all because of bitches like you, an you're here beggin for your life, you ain't no fuckin gangsta. Pussy you shouldn't be carryin feelings, I robbed your niggas their bitches, you should have left it like dat. Do you know they fuckin gave up your brown to me without me pullin my fuckin strap, pussies; and now you're gonna die over their weakness and your fuckin mistake."

Same time Blacka's phone vibrated. Thinking it's one of the man dem he took out his phone to answer. For a split second he went into a trance, Mya's name flashed on the screen. I felt a change in his pulse, his aura felt different, he was a fool. I was willing to forgive his wrongs, forget his sins, his transgression, and let it slip. I had lost Blacka to this preacher. It was clear in his heart; he knew she could offer what I could never, which was physical comfort and companionship that led to reproduction, and not the destructive slow path of the discontinuation of mankind's existence. He no longer wanted me, or the path of destruction, he wanted out of the game. His dealings with Rogerton were just unfinished business, his next move wasn't out of loyalty to me and our covenant, but to his cousin and friends, and his foolish pride which I once delighted in. Blacka shoved the phone back in his pocket.

"Dead pussy." Blacka shouted as he squeezed the trigger. I refrained from firing, I held back mine, jamming myself. He squeezed and squeezed, my counter pressure withheld my army of men, who at one time would be more than willing to sink their claws into mortal flesh, and return man to the dust from whence they came.

We were no longer companions of destruction; we were on two different teams.

Knowing the gun was jammed Rogerton threw himself at Blacka grabbing him around the waist. At this point Blacka had dropped me and reached for the gun he had taken off Rogerton, but Rogerton had a similar idea and sucked onto him trapping Blacka's hand behind him as he wrestled him to the ground. Blacka landed on his arm, injuring his shoulder. With one arm trapped Blacka was surely at a disadvantage. They scuffled for a few seconds, when suddenly Blacka screamed out. Rogerton pulled the hand out that had trapped Blacka's arm behind him and came out with his strap that Blacka had shoved down the back of his pants. As he stood up his other hand held a blade that dripped with Blacka's blood.

Blacka lay on the floor staring up at Rogerton as he held his belly.

"Dead pussy," Rogerton said angrily. "Who's the dead man now, pussy?" he pointed his gun at him. "Tek out your phone, dash it on da floor pussy." Rogerton picked it up. "You don't need dis where you're going." He smiled an evil grin.

Rogerton had stabbed Blacka in the left side of his torso. So much for Blacka's search for weapons, he had disarmed him of his gun, a thorough search would have led him to find Rogerton's knife. Blacka was slipping in every aspect of the word streetwise. A quick pat down made the difference between life and death. He had slipped and now fallen to his own doings.

Blacka stared at me as I lay on the floor not too far away. I was reachable, well maybe if he didn't have someone standing over him with a gun pointed at his chest. "Arrhh," he groaned as Rogerton kicked him in his face.

"Don't even think about it." Rogerton picked me up. I felt his desire, his want, and his determination to kill, to take life and shed blood. I instantly believed and surrendered myself; after all, Blacka had no use to me anymore, he was soon to be a dead man.

Blacka began to crawl away.

"Where the fuck you think you're going?" Rogerton kicked him in his ribs, and stamped on him multiple times. Blacka grunted. "Turn over pussy."

Helplessly he lay there compressing the wounds on the left side of his body, his other hand he raised over his face. Blacka's actions surprised me, of all the people who used my kind frequently, Blacka should know the power we guns possess, as if mortal flesh could prevent bullets boring through the bone structure of his face. I guess the thought of a closed casket funeral wasn't Blacka's first option.

"What you covering your face for, pussy." Rogerton's warmth and firm grip that encompassed my cold frame, comforted me, I felt needed. My allegiance was made. Rogerton squeezed. I am the commander of my vessel, there's no smoke without fire, and I come with both. With no regard for the covenant we once shared, I came at Blacka as if he was a stray dog that needed to be put down. He felt instant warmth as I penetrated through his flesh removing tissue from my path as I entered his abdomen. Blacka's eyes opened wide, he raised both hands as if he was praying out to the Lord. No-one was coming to save him.

Rogerton stood there pointing two guns at Blacka. Blacka lay there looking up at me, he took no notice of the other gun, it was as if he had gone into a trance, his eyes showed betrayal, as he glared into my nozzle.

The sweet aroma somewhat pleasant like personified perfume was no longer his to enjoy. Never again was he going to be behind my trigger, or any trigger in fact. He was on the opposite side of the fence. They say the grass looks greener on the other side. I doubt Blacka would agree.

I had given him power, name and credibility on the streets, yet he had betrayed, abused and angered me. Surely a faithful servant would respect and appreciate his master who protects, feeds, and clothes him, but not Blacka. Together we had robbed, killed and injured many, his blood stained hands had given testimony of my power. Now on the receiving end he bared witness of my strength. I had ripped into his abdominal wall, smoothly and easily I glided through mortal flesh.

"You're owna gun gonna kill you tonight, pussy." Rogerton required my assistance for a second time.

Fear entered Blacka's dull eyes once again, as he opened his eyes wide as I pierced a hole in his sternum. The ever familiar noise of my shout weakened his spirit. Oh, how the mighty have fallen, fainthearted he has become.

"Done playin games." He pointed me at him

"Don't kill me," said blacka. Blood spewed from his mouth as he spoke. From the corner of his mouth dripped discoloured blood onto his garments.

A now weakened warrior begged for his life. No one but Blacka had chosen this life for him, his path, his doings; he had lured himself to his own death. There are innocent, and there are innocent, but Blacka was neither. He had killed, and murdered time after time. So you live so you die.

It amazed me how mankind are so willing to do harm and hate to have it being done to themselves. How wrath is so easily dished out as if it was a fine cuisine, yet when on the receiving end, not so easily digested.

Blacka's chest moved rapidly as he struggled to breathe, grasping for breath like a fish out of water, his place of belonging was slowly coming to an end.

"You done beg?" Rogerton laughed. His blood bubbled, I felt the pulse in his finger give evidence of his thought, he was going to command me again, I was going to finish off that helpless dog once and for all. I knew my killing spree with Rogerton had just begun. Suddenly he redirected me; I welcomed the challenge with an answer of my own.

From a distance Shaggy and Dean were firing at us. He who runs away lives to fight another day said Robert Nesta Marley, and he was right. We were out gunned. Two against one, the odds were in their favour. My new master and I disappeared into the dark.

Surely, this wouldn't be the last time those two fucking cunts would see me. We will meet again. Shaggy had wished me gone on numerous occasions; oh, I will get him, as I got Blacka, and would have killed his right hand Danger if he had not given his life away to someone else. No one turns their back on me, no one.

"Bloodclaat, gangsta," said Shaggy as he knelt down and held blacka.

"Fuck nah man," Dean breathed heavily as tears came to his eyes. "Stay wid us blud." Dean put his hand on his head. He lowered his hand and then went into his pocket and took out his phone.

"Wah yu ah do, yuh ah mad man? Yu nah tink my yout, yu dial 999 yu jus get fuck. Yu forget seh ah contract phone yu ave?"

"Get his phone out of his pocket, call an ambulance," Dean responded with panic in his tone.

"Can't find it," answered Shaggy.

"Use yours blud, it's a pay as you go."

"Mi nah carry phone pon works my yout, dat tun off and left inna da yard. Yo Blacka, fight it my yout, fight it."

Blacka coughed up dark blood; the blood that came from Blacka's mouth thickened and was accompanied by clotting factors. The wounds were to servere, damage had been done to vital organs. Blacka's body shook relentlessly as the cold set in, his system no longer regulated, and his core temperature dropped.

"Bombaclaat. Blacka, my yout." Shaggy murmured.

The noise of sirens caused Dean and Shaggy to look at one another. Blacka griped shaggy's jacket. Struggling to speak as blood blocked his airways; he made noises and grunted, blood spewed from his mouth, in an almost whispering tone he cried, "Mya."

Dean shook his head.

"Don't talk my yout, save yuh breathe, Mya alright," Shaggy responded.

Shaggy shook his head at Dean; the look in his eyes said it all. Blacka was never gonna make it, and time was ticking; police were drawing near. They weren't willing to risk tempting fate twice with regards to escaping police; they needed to leave, and needed to leave like right now. Not wanting to abandon Blacka, but they knew that if they stayed around, Bonso and Cha Chu wouldn't be the only ones facing a life sentence, not to mention Ticka and Blacka would have died in vain.

This vicious cycle of death seems like it would never end. To regroup and retaliate was the motive without question.

Blacka watched as his friends disappeared out of sight. He was alone. They say during your dying movement your whole life flashes before you, whoever said so was absolutely correct. Thoughts of Mya, Danger, Cassandra and his nephew Melekiah, his life and how he lived it ran through his mind. Street life for himself was merely a choice, chosen by the delusional portrait which made badness seem the norm. Media had played its role in Blacka's demise, but then so did the older generation. The reality of Dangers message began to sink in. Flashbacks of Danger's smile after his statement about dying gracefully, greeting death like a fat pussy gal, which Blacka was unable to do, troubled him. Death followed this lifestyle, but Blacka wasn't prepared or willing to greet it; he didn't want to die. Blacka had always thought Danger had not lived life as a gangster by choice, but due to his permit and illegal issues. He now knew he was wrong, he realized at that moment there was always a choice and the consequences of our choices are what we have to live with. As Blacka lay there dying, it dawned on him, Danger had made a choice due to his circumstance, and suddenly realized Danger could have waited no matter how long and hard it may have been, but he had made a choice. He recalled Danger saying when his papers came through he was going to give it up, he loved family life, but was driven to provide at the same time. It took death for Blacka to see life. He realised his circumstance wasn't the same as Danger's, but like Danger and many other street soldier's they all had a choice and chose the selfish path, which really is a dark road to nowhere. Thoughts caused tears to flow from his eyes; he knew Cassandra and Melekiah would now have to fend for themselves. Blinded by his own selfish desires, he had come to realise that instead of helping the situation, in the long term he had only made things worse for the people that loved him.

Fighting with himself he lay there trying to breathe, praying to cough up the blood that clogged deep in his airways, just to bid him a minute longer. Surely blood is the life of the body; this was definitely a true statement. Blacka wrestled with his spirit, not willing for it to depart from his body, he wanted more time.

It's funny thought Blacka only during my dying moments I realised that a man should never say he has done or gone too far to turn back, it's just the lack of will to pick up and re-adjust oneself. He knew he would never have that chance, and only wished he could have said his thoughts to Dean and Shaggy. He knew they were never going to leave this beef with Rogerton alone. Blacka now saw the endless killing, the reality of which Mya feared. As a street man, he also understood, that it's harder to come to grips with reality when one is in the circle, it's only when you step out and look back or at everything within, that you realise it's more trouble than it's worth. But the problem was how many were willing to step out of an illusion clothed so beautifully. Vanity and vain images were at the root of the violence amongst our people. Everyone knows wrong from right, but when wrong is dressed to look appealing, hell will lure you into its gates.

The black on black violence which tormented our communities; things were not always like this. He recalled his youthful days, when community spirit was at the heart of Harlesden, South Kilburn, and surrounding areas, and the violence amongst our people wasn't as high. At that time society offered so much to the youth. Now, there was nothing for them to do, nowhere for them to go. Street corners were now their only meeting places. Neglect and divide, added together with a deep lack of self-knowledge, triggered our people to self terminate. Like a time bomb, we were set to blow, and what saddened Blacka most during his last moments, was that he only saw things getting worst. Such thoughts hurt Blacka more than the wounds of his flesh, they were more painful than the thought of self hate, for without knowledge of self one could never truly love.

A people with no true knowledge of where they're coming from, could never really know where they are going. In such state of mind, it is simple, and technically easier to manipulate a people to remain absent of the knowledge of their worth, to divide the nation, play their women against their men, their children against their parents, and their men against one another. Mya believed I could have done better with myself and my life, and I agree, but now it was too late to find out what I could have done, or maybe have become. One thing I knew I was dying, and if I could have relived my life, well; I guess I would change the way I chose to live in a heartbeat he thought.

Blacka stopped thinking for a second, in his blurred vision he saw police officers approaching. I guess this is my last heartbeat. Blacka died that very second, blooded, cold and alone.

Epilogue

Snuggled between his sheet and the warmth of his body heat penetrating through his pillow, I felt comforted, needed and desired. Rogerton was taking no chances. From the moment he touched me, we bonded, upon firing me, a new covenant was made. He chose me, his other gun, he placed on the bedside table, but me he kept me close, and I'll keep him closer.

With Shaggy and Dean still alive, Rogerton and I knew we would always be at war with them. It bothered me not. I was made to confront battle and so will I do because it's my nature. Death accompanies me, destruction is all I know. I was made to terminate life, period. I am what I am, and I do that which I was made to do. After all, I'm a fucking gun.

STEPHEN GRAHAM

I'M A
GUN
TOO

COMING SOON
www.expressivelypassionate.com

Printed in Great Britain
by Amazon.co.uk, Ltd.,
Marston Gate.